COLLISION

Book II

Michael Phillip Cash

Disclaimer

The characters and events portrayed in this book are fictitious. Any resemblance to real persons, living or dead, on Earth or Darracia, is coincidental and not intended by the author.

No part of this book may be reproduced, or stored in a retrieval system, or transmitted in any form or by any means, electronic or mechanical, including photocopying, recording, or otherwise, without the express written permission of the publisher.

Published in the United States by Red Feather Publishing

New York • Los Angeles • Las Vegas All rights reserved.

ISBN-10: 1-947118-75-7

ISBN-13: 978-1-947118-75-1

col·li·sion *noun* \kə'liZHən\

1. an instance of one moving object or person striking violently against another. When you're drowning, you don't say "I would be incredibly pleased if someone would have the foresight to notice me drowning and come and help me." You just scream.

—John Lennon

Other Books by Michael Phillip Cash

Brood X: A Firsthand Account of the Great Cicada Invasion

Stillwell: A Haunting on Long Island

The Hanging Tree: A Novella

The Flip

The After House

Witches Protection Program

Pokergeist

I

THE SHORES OF Fon Reni were fine black sand dotted with purple sea glass that littered the barren beach. Stars littered the velvet sky; here and there a shooting cosmic spray spread across the inky darkness, illuminating the still night. It was quiet here, the distant planet devoid of life, save the lonely inhabitants who lived on the beach, footprints washed away by the icy seas.

He had constructed a crude hut for his guest using the fronds on the leafy trees that populated the jungles. Zayden slept under the night stars, enjoying the peaceful freedom of the beach. Living on what he hunted, he reveled in the quiet of Fon Reni, knowing it was far from Darracia, his troubles, and the memories. He was tired, exhausted by grief, angry with his lack of solution.

Staf Nuen had disappeared. It was as though he had never existed. Zayden had spent almost a year tracking him, coming up with nothing but dead ends. He had traveled from one end of the solar system to the other, living by his wits, surviving hand to mouth, always just missing him. He must have gotten close, because he was jumped outside a graphen den on the planet Venturian.

He woke up disoriented, shamefaced, with his new-found friend, Denita, and with a colorful tattoo on his biceps. He watched the ripples rise from the dark sand, the heat sucking the air from his lungs. It was as hot as a furnace. He wore just his trousers, naked from the waist up, so he could see the stupid tattoo taking up most of his shoulder. The bruises on his torso had faded a bit, but his face still looked as battered as an old suitcase. Sweat evaporated as soon as it appeared, and he let the hot air roast him. He heard the foliage rustle behind him, made a face, then laughed softly at the curse he heard muttered behind the screen of the dense brush.

There were fourteen planets in his solar system, Darracia being his native one. He had left it in search of his uncle Staf Nuen, who had killed his father, King Drakko, leaving his legitimate half brother, V'sair, the reigning king. V'sair pleaded with him to stay as his advisor, Zayden remembered, rubbing the still-raw scar that bisected his once-handsome face. The new king had appointed him grand mestor, Zayden thought with chagrin. Imagine that, the bastard of King Drakko was offered the highest position in the land.

He drew aimlessly in the dark sand with a broken stick. He didn't want it. He didn't want any part of it until he could bring Staf Nuen to justice. It was because of his uncle's overthrow that his beloved Hilde was slain, killed by her psychotic brother when she protected Zayden from the deathblow of a Fireblade. Clenching his hands into useless fists, he relived the last moments of her life. The empty socket where his amber eye used to be throbbed as though a thousand pickaxes were stabbing it. Pressing deeply with his palms, he covered his eyes, trying to blot out the images imprinted on his brain: blood, blood, and more blood, coupled with Hilde's dying gasp as she collapsed into his arms, a sword robbing him of his future with the only woman he ever felt he could love.

He glanced at his discarded Fireblade, thrown negligently on the sandy ground. He hadn't used it since that day, preferring the heavy pistol strapped to the side of his leg. Darracians disdained guns. Swords were for warriors, guns for cowards, he had been taught. His people valued the skill one developed with a blade, never respecting those beings who just aimed and fired. Guns were illegal at home, the punishment fierce if one was caught with such a firearm. His father had taught him it was dishonorable; if a warrior fought in combat, he must be engaged with his opponent, feel the heat of battle. Guns made warfare impersonal; there was no honor to kill without knowing the skill of your enemy. It showed lack of respect for the ideals of battle. That was why only a small part of the population knew how to fight with the Fireblade—it kept violence at a minimum. Darracian warriors were taught to uphold justice, never kill for personal gain, and until his uncle had tried to overthrow the government, Darracia had been a relatively mild place to live. He had picked up the gun on the lawless space station Pagil 7, far from the rules of Darracia.

After V'sair had rocked the foundation of the beliefs about the Fireblade, Zayden didn't want it anymore. It seemed that Darracians had gotten it all wrong. Chanters from all over his former home were meeting, trying to make sense out of the Sradda Doctriness. There were forums and debates; all the schools were rereading and trying to find new ways to interpret the messages of the Elements. Well, he didn't give a crap about all that religious stuff. His faith died when Hilde perished. He didn't know why he hadn't jettisoned the Fireblade from his portal as he traveled through deep space. He shrugged his broad shoulders, thinking perhaps because it was presented to him by his late father when he achieved his highest honors, and he was a sentimental fool, after all. He felt naked without it. He eyed his sword with resentment. Denita should never have taken it from the thug who tried to kill him. She should have left both him and the Fireblade to rot on the filthy streets of Venturian. Zayden sighed gustily. So here he sat, on the desolate beach of Fon Reni, reliving his nightmare and waiting for a sign— a signal for him to find Staf Nuen and kill him with his bare hands.

He watched the progress of the silver crabs as they clawed their way up the dark sand of the beach. The tiny feet worked in unison, scrabbling through dense patches of seaweed. There were hundreds of them. He tapped his stick thoughtfully. Well, he wouldn't have to work very hard for their dinner tonight. Pushing himself onto his feet, he stretched widely, feeling his cramped muscles expand and his bones crack. His head still ached where he'd been beaten, and his ribs reminded him they weren't all that healed after all. He grabbed a rush basket and then began to pluck the crabs from the ground until his container was a swirling mass of nervous creatures trying to escape. He placed them over the fire he had built earlier, in an old helmet he used as a pot. Soon, he heard the crackle and hiss of their bursting shells, their color changing to an appetizing light green. He thought to call out that dinner was ready, but shrugged instead, plopping down on the sand to eat alone. That's how he wanted to eat, by himself. His guest was nothing more than an encumbrance. He sneered at the dense forest behind him. Carefully, he pulled a cooked crab out of his makeshift pot, singeing his fingers, catching the green juice of the dripping crustacean with his tongue.

The fire warmed him against the stiff ocean breeze, and memories of camping trips with his father and V'sair came rushing back like a tidal wave. They had stayed here, the three of them, on this very beach. V'sair was so young, his royal braid barely touching his shoulder. No servants were allowed, and though his father's elite guards hovered in the sky above, they spent a sun-filled week on Fon Reni that became a yearly ritual. They returned V'sair, to his mother's horror, a lovely shade of brown, his light-tannish-blue skin burned and toughened by the strong rays of both suns. It was a special spot for Zayden. Here he was just Drakko's son and V'sair's older brother, not the illegitimate offspring of the king and his laundress.

He had loved his father, as well as his royal younger brother, despite the differences in their stations, even though it appeared that he was the only one troubled by it. He was older by a good fifteen years, and he didn't begrudge his younger sibling his inheritance; however, sometimes he admitted to himself that he felt invisible. It was funny, he mused, V'sair envied Zayden's Darracian strength, and he valued what V'sair took most for granted, his assured place in Darracian hierarchy. Oh, V'sair always treated him with respect, had offered him the position of grand mestor, but Zayden knew what the others felt. He was seen as an interloper, barely tolerated despite the fact that he was one of the army's fiercest warriors.

He constantly pushed himself to be faster with his Fireblade, the hardest rider when it came to his stallius, as well as the best jolter in the tournaments. He lived by his warrior's creed, happy to make his father proud. He enjoyed showing them all his royal placement was earned with dedication and hard work. But somehow the dynamics of the Fireblade had changed now. It was not about brute strength and chivalry, so where did it leave him? He reached over to grab his sword and heard it hum to life, great red streaks lighting with energy. He knew now it was the wrong color. It was the shade of anger, not strength. Once, it had been the true blue of justice and a force to be reckoned with. His had always been the blue of a pure heart, even though he never realized what it meant. Now it blazed red, like his enemy's. The Fireblade was about something else now, and he didn't have the patience to try to understand. He was too tired.

Angry and tired.

He threw the shells of his crab onto a neat pile, sucking the meat from the tiny claws. He should eat all of them, he thought with a mean chuckle. She had missed their nightly progress; Denita never learned. He eyed the last few crabs and groaned. Last time she had walked in the shallow waters, she had cut her foot. No, it wasn't worth it—he'd have to nurse her again and hear her complaints. She could be an ornery pain in the ass. Better leave her enough to satisfy her hunger. He tried to remember Hilde's soft laughter, and Denita's velvet voice smothered the ladylike sound. Instead he pulled a frayed black ribbon from a pouch and held it to his nose. Her scent was gone. Just like Hilde. Gone forever. None of that mattered now anyway. The one he wanted more than life was taken from him this last year, killed by the hand of her brother, Pacuto. Zayden could not rest until he brought her traitorous father to justice.

The four moons lit the beach, bathing him in their glow. He watched phosphorus mengles dance under the waves, their multicolored poison glowing iridescently under the swirling sea. Swimming was out of the question. One sting from their tails and he would sink to the bottom of the water, never to be seen again. He drank deeply from a flask, swallowing the burn of the liquor, his eye never leaving the horizon of the endless ocean. Then what would his guest do, he thought contemptuously. He needed this complication the way one needed a headache. She would do nothing but slow him down, and although they had a common hatred for Staf Nuen, Zayden had parked himself here hoping she'd lose interest. Denita had howled with outrage when he landed, screaming for him to proceed to Planta and find his uncle. He didn't need her or anyone else. He didn't want her or anyone else, for that matter.

He eyed the circular mark on his upper bicep. It didn't hurt anymore, and he supposed Reminda would know someone who could get rid of it. As much as he hated it, he thought he'd keep it now. It was just another scar, like his ruined face, marked on this journey for revenge. Taking a faded patch from his pocket, he covered the empty place where his eye used to be. A comet streaked across the sky. He searched his memory for its name and came up with nothing. Due to his fight patterns, he knew every celestial event in the sky. Hearing about this one must have escaped him. He watched its progress, its feathered tail stretched out for miles, curving toward the west. Comets always meant something. Emmicus, his old tutor, always said that. Something was going to happen, he thought, wiping the back of his hand against his mouth. The salt and sand burned against his lips. He scanned the stygian sky. Yes, something was coming. He just wasn't sure of when or what.

II

V'SAIR, THE YOUNG king of Darracia, stared pensively out of the window wall from his private chamber. It was the place he loved most in his castle, where he had spent many peaceful hours studying with his navigator, Emmicus. Leaning his head against the cool glass, he looked down on the Desa below, wondering where Tulani was now.

Aqin, the ancient volcano, was dormant again, and Quyroos were stubbornly rebuilding their homes on its craggy surface. A light mist created a wall of clouds that obscured the landscape. The air felt thick, the city strangely silent. The dense fog muted the sounds of traffic. The city of Syos looked peaceful, the forest of the Desa, not so much, and V'sair, not at all.

Nothing had worked right since he was crowned. His father had been the driving force for tolerance of the

Quyroos. Without him, getting everybody to the Moon Council had been almost impossible. First there had been several months of mourning. So many had been killed. Barely a clan on Darracia had not suffered. Those who sided with his uncle languished in prison, cutting his armed forces in half. In the spirit of equality, he had invited the Quyroos to join up. He was unprepared for the blatant hostility between the two species. While his father sought to usher in an age of peace and understanding, V'sair was bequeathed a planet divided by prejudice and distrust. He wanted to change things, to bring the equality and peace he knew deep in his heart was the right way for his home.

General Swart accused him of rushing these new laws. The older man was insecure with so small a fighting force. They had argued about importing large cannon. Swart wanted to modernize the army; V'sair would not have it. Swart had taken his place as V'sair's grand mestor, his advisor, and though he was loyal unto death, he was no friend to his late father's policies. He wanted to build up the army and go after the prince's nefarious uncle Staf Nuen. Eliminate the threat of invasion, then fix the problems at home, he had urged the young king.

While V'sair knew his uncle was still out there, planning something, the pressing problems of unrest lay heavy on his young shoulders. He missed his father's quiet strength; he missed his brother's support; he missed Tulani's unconditional love. He was bereft.

His heart melted when he thought of Tulani. They had known each other forever, but he realized what she meant to him only when they learned the secrets of the Fireblade together. When his cousin had threatened her with bodily harm, he discovered he was capable of a killing rage that filled him with white-hot lava. His heart and mind knew Tulani, and he felt connected to her in a way he had never experienced before. When the good general had brought up a marriage alliance with a princess of another planet, V'sair silenced his grand mestor with royal finality. He wanted no one but the Quyroo high priestess. Tulani was as much a part of him as his arm or eyes. He would wait forever until they could find peace in each other's arms.

The warm, wet tongue of Felise bathed his hand. Twining his fingers in the curly black hair on the top of her head, he looked down, a smile tugging at his lips at her mournful eyes. His mother had gifted him with a newborn jast mere days after his father was murdered. His pet was a mess, nervous to be separated from her litter, her clumsy paws tracking in the red dust that always drifted onto the balconies. Felise rubbed her wiry whiskers against his palm, demanding attention in her selfish way. She panted, leaping onto her hind legs, her front paws resting easily on his shoulders, and a laugh escaped his lips. She was not tiny anymore, and a rather big nuisance as well, because while his pet was really still an infant, she had grown to almost half her adult size, and an awesome size it was too.

He heard the door open and knew it was his mother from her light footsteps. Felise drooled sloppily as she greeted the queen.

"Walk with me, Vsos." She came up behind him and rested her hand on his back. He directed Felise to sit with a stern stare and heard his mother chuckle. "Silly beast," she said fondly, patting her head.

"It's cold outside," he responded, looking straight ahead.

"I don't care. The fresh air will do you good. I heard that it has stopped raining." He caught her intense gaze. "You are not eating enough, Vsos."

The king shrugged. "I am not hungry."

"I think Felise is eating enough for both of you." She smiled and scratched the giant animal beneath the soft curls of her chin. She turned and rested her hand in the crook of V'sair's elbow. Her white hair was threaded with black strands now. She had aged since losing her husband. Lines had formed around her iridescent eyes, bracketed her oncelush lips, giving her the appearance of a constant frown.

"Tulani would not know you, my son."

"Doesn't make a difference, since she won't come here."

The portal swooshed open, and they stepped onto the balcony connected to the room. They heard the giant jast follow them, her paws clicking on the wet tiled floor. Two Quyroo guards stood on either side of them, their impassive faces glued to the horizon. The interminable rain had ceased, but it was still overcast; weak sunlight fought to peek through the clouds.

"You have to allow her time."

"Time for what?" V'sair answered hotly. "Anything she can do there"—he pointed a long bluish finger down at the forests—"can be done from here." His eyes blazed with anger.

"She feels she is doing you more good down there"—Reminda gestured to the dark planet—"than here. She is the best ambassador you could have."

V'sair clicked impatiently with his tongue. "I have shuttles full of willing Quyroos that desire to be ambassadors. We could unite this planet if she were queen!"

"Yes." Reminda placed a thoughtful finger next to her temple. "Consider her place, V'sair. You above anyone else should be able to commiserate with her feelings. She is neither Darracian nor Quyroo."

"She is full-blooded Quyroo!" V'sair shot back, interrupting her.

"True," Reminda said reasonably, "but taken to live among us at three years of age. She can't be seen as one of them until she is accepted by them. Tulani understood for this to succeed, she must gain their confidence and then take her place by your side. Vsos, I don't understand; usually you are the most amiable of creatures."

"This is harder than I thought." V'sair pulled her by her hand to walk the parapets, far from the guards. "I don't know if I can do this anymore. I don't know if I want to do this."

"V'sair, this is your destiny," Reminda told him urgently. "Even Ozre told you that. I...I never expected this to be thrust on you so early. Your father and I still had so much work to do, but"—she shrugged, her eyes glittering with unshed tears—"this is what it is, and we have to make do with what we have."

"It is a test, but for what I don't know," V'sair told her absently. "I just wish Tulani were here with me, Mo'mo. She is my rock."

"She needs to finish what she has started. Being a priestess is complicated. She must learn how to use her power."

"Pah!" V'sair clicked his tongue. "If I were not king and she not a daughter of Nost, we could be together. This life you chose for me has become a burden. I wish Dado was here."

Reminda sighed, eyeing her son sadly. "We did not expect you to have to take the throne until you were much older. Your father had plans; he wanted to teach you many things."

"I don't know how to do this. The Quyroos are unhappy; the Darracians are unhappy; I am unhappy. This is hard, Mo'mo. I don't know how to make them get along."

"Patience. You have never learned patience."

V'sair rested his hands on the terrace wall, his face scanning the vast city spread out before him. "First Zayden runs off to slay his dragon, when I need him here. Then Tulani discovers she must learn about her Desa and make the Quyroos love her, before she can commit. What about me?" he demanded, turning to face his mother. "I need their help." "Well, at least you have me," she told him with a smile and a quick shrug.

"Oh aye, I am sorry, Mo'mo. I am being unreasonable." He looked at her sheepishly, a lock of white hair falling over his blue eyes. "It's just that…it…"

He looked so young; Reminda's heart softened. She reached out to push his hair from his eyes, thought better of it, and smiled gently. "Dado is gone. Emmicus as well. I know it's hard, Vsos, but everybody's life has been changed. The New Doctrines have shaken Darracian society to its core. You have to give everything time."

The whole of Darracia had been turned upside down, Reminda thought ruefully. Such a lot of nonsense simply because V'sair had shown them that the Fireblade could be earned and used by all. Darracians were not special, their superiority not guaranteed, and the whole species now had to relearn to fire their blades to the blue of courage and justice, rather than the red of anger and intolerance. Schools had shut down, chanters met for conferences, creating new interpretations and criteria so that all the inhabitants of this planet could share its bounty to live as equals with the same opportunities.

But there was opposition. Many clans stayed away from court, keeping their Darracian sons and daughters from mixing with the Quyroos who now were finding new positions other than the serving class. Why, just the other day, she had heard that a wealthy merchant had disowned his daughter for marrying a Quyroo communications officer. These new customs were going to take time. She looked at the fine lines of worry on her son's face. Both she and Drakko had wanted to bring about the changes slowly, not thrust them on her teenage son. And, she wondered angrily, where were the Elements? Why did they topple the old beliefs and then simply go silent? It made no sense.

"Have you asked the Elements for guidance?"

V'sair turned to look at the city again, his eyes distant.

He shrugged. "Yes, of course. They never tell you anything." He added sarcastically, "They wait for you to have the *illumination*."

"So, did you?" his mother asked.

"Yes, yes, Mother. I understand that we all have to look inside of ourselves to find our strength."

"And…"

"Well, I've done that already," he added indignantly.

"That's very nice, but what about Zayden and Tulani?"

V'sair didn't answer for a moment. He sighed and looked at his mother, his face relaxing. "I know, Mo'mo. Just because I have found myself, I have to allow the others to catch up to me. I didn't say I have to like it."

Reminda smiled and squeezed his arm. "I know it feels like forever, but it will really be a very short part of your life, this waiting. What is it, V'sair?" Reminda saw his lips turn down in a thoughtful frown.

"Ozre."

"Go on."

"I am concerned. I have not heard from him in months."

"Perhaps you are not praying hard enough?"

V'sair gave her a sidelong look. "Me? Oh, I pray hard enough."

"Maybe you are praying for the wrong things?" his mother asked gently.

V'sair didn't answer, his eyes searching the Desa. The red canopy of trees shielded the Desa floor from prying eyes; he could see nothing through the tangled forest. The wet treetops glittered as if they were dusted with rubies. Still, he watched, wishing he could see

Tulani and know that she was ready to join him. His fisted palm absently pounded the balustrade. Felise jumped up, pushing next to him. V'sair grinned, knowing the jast was watching him; he let himself lean into her strong shoulder.

From the rear, they looked as if they were two friends looking out on the city. Reminda smiled at his shortened white braid. It was what marked him as a Darracian royal. It would take a while until it grew back. His cousin Pacuto had hacked it off in a fight.

"Get down, you pestilent beast." His mother playfully hit Felise on her back. "You spoil her, Vsos. She shouldn't be out here."

"She was your idea."

"I thought you might need a friend," Reminda told him, then added softly, "I know I did."

"You miss him, Mo'mo."

"You have no idea, Vsos. It's like there is a great hole inside of me." She grew quiet, examining the dark plains of her son's face. He was all sharp angles; the sweet softness of youth had disappeared with his lost innocence. He was not the same since his father's murder. None of them were. His boyhood had flown with the destruction of her dreams. "Such is life, Vsos. We are born, we serve, and then our anima leaves." "Our anima?"

"Your soul."

"A rather empty existence, don't you think?"

"I would give up ten lifetimes to have shared what I did with your father, Vsos. I discarded everything I knew for him—my home, my family." She turned to face him.

"And he gave me you. And you gave me Tulani." She looked out at the Desa, her iridescent eyes narrowing. "Now if only she would finish what she needs to do, come back here, and give me some grandchildren."

"Yes," V'sair agreed. "If only."

"Have you thought about the coronation?" Reminda asked briskly, trying to change the mood. She observed her son's strong shoulders, the light growth of a white beard on his chin. He was no longer a pliable child. This topic was a sore spot. V'sair first refused the ceremony due to the depth of mourning in the court. Many times General Swart had brought it up, but V'sair clearly wasn't interested. Reminda knew it was something he must do, but now her son could not be forced.

"It feels strange, Mother. I don't know if I am ready for it."

"Your father would have wanted you to be crowned," she told him. "This is our way; you were born to be his successor," she added fiercely.

"It doesn't feel right." V'sair looked back at the dormant volcano, his eyes distant.

"He is not coming back, Vsos. You must declare your place."

"I will consider it, Mo'mo," he responded forlornly. They stood together watching the day wane and the four moons of Darracia climb the horizon. Gresh chirped their mournful love call nearby, while they both sat in comfortable silence.

"Are you hungry yet?" Reminda asked, ever the mother.

"I suppose," V'sair answered, distracted by a

spinning luminescence in the growing twilight. Felise barked loudly at it, racing down the balcony, chasing the blazing light. He followed the comet's arc. "Fon Reni," he said softly. A thought struck him, and he suddenly knew where his half brother had gone. His blue eyes lit up for the first time in weeks.

"What is it?" Reminda asked.

"That's where my brother is," he remarked with wonder as he watched the comet's tail light up the night sky. "He must be there. It is where I would go if I could. That's where he's staying. He went to Fon Reni—he loves it there."

"Will you go to him?"

"No." V'sair shook his head. "I can't leave here."

"Surely, for a few days…"

"No, Mo'mo." He sighed heavily. "There is too much unrest. There was an incident…"

"Oh." Reminda raised a delicate eyebrow. "I hadn't heard."

"I just got the report. General Swart captured a group of malcontents."

"Go on," Reminda urged.

"They were plotting an assassination. I didn't want you to know."

Reminda gasped, her face paling.

"Oh, Mo'mo. There was no reason to alarm you. We have it all under control. It's just the…the people are so very unhappy." V'sair looked miserable.

Oh Drakko, Reminda thought sadly, *what have we bequeathed to our son? Why couldn't we just run away and make a life for ourselves? Why did we decide to take on the world and change it?*

"Please don't worry. It's been handled." V'sair gave his mother a lopsided grin. "You know it comes with the job description. Besides, if Zayden is there, he wants to be alone. He is working things out, and once he finds what he needs, he will come home."

"You are so sure?" Reminda knew she was going to try to find a way to contact Zayden. His brother needed him now. Enough of his self-pity, she needed him to protect her son, his king.

"I know Zayden. He loves Fon Reni. You never saw that side of him when we were there. Fon Reni is his spot. You understand?" V'sair asked.

Reminda nodded her head. "Yes."

"If he is there, he will find his peace."

"What if he doesn't?"

"He will not return until he does," V'sair told her with finality. His breath caught in his chest, and he touched the area over his heart. "He will be coming home, I think. No…I know. He will be coming soon."

"You see. I told you things will fall into place." Reminda didn't know if she was assuring her son or herself.

"Soon," V'sair answered her absently. "Yes, soon."

They entered the castle, walking arm in arm to the throne room, Felise trailing after them. The fire blazed, its incandescence throwing sparks behind the giant fire screen he had installed after his mother and aunt had rolled into the blaze. It heated the room mightily, but a dart of apprehension curled up V'sair's spine, making him shiver involuntarily.

"What is it?" his mother asked anxiously, her concerned eyes searching his face.

"I don't know. I felt something, just for a minute."

"What?" she asked, her voice a mere whisper over the soft music playing in the room.

V'sair's eyes scanned the many groups clustered in the room. It was a court still in mourning. So many of them had lost members of their families when his uncle engineered a coup taking over the planet and killing his father. No one wore anything but white, the official color of mourning. Even the armed forces still wore the badge of white on their sleeves to mark that the year had not ended. Though Quyroos were invited, they rarely came to his court. The Darracians barely tolerated them. Old wounds healed slowly. "A feeling, Mo'mo. Just a feeling." He narrowed his gaze.

"As though someone just danced on my grave."

"Stop!" Reminda took his hands. "Don't even think like that. Come," she snapped at the musician, "play something lively. This court has had enough sadness." She held up her webbed hand to stop him. "No, wait, we have mourned enough. It is time to cast off our whites." She motioned to her new serving girl. "Come, Tosha. Attend me. I will change." She looked hard at her son. "It's time to move forward with your father's plans. I will be right back. Do not speak of graves to me again, my son."

The flutist looked at the king, who nodded his

head, and the music took on a light, playful sound. Conversations picked up, and Reminda smiled.

"You will excuse me, Your Majesty." She curtsied solemnly.

V'sair bowed deeply. "As you wish, Mother." He watched her leave the room, followed by a group of chattering females excited to wear colors once again.

He looked at the thinned lips and impatient glare of General Swart, took a deep breath, and tried to dispel his unease. He strolled over to his throne and sat down. Felise flopped at his feet, her cheeks resting on his thigh while he absently stroked her head. For his mother's sake, he would not mention it again, but while they could get rid of the mourning white, no amount of color was going to make this feeling of foreboding go away.

III

TULANI ROLLED ON the floor, her arms crusted with dirt and a bit of red mud. She was in a circle, naked save for her loincloth, which was torn and matted with dried blood. A steady drizzle had turned the red dust to a viscous mud that coated everything. It was twice as hard to fight in the slippery muck, and Tulani had the wounds to prove its danger. Long scratches grazed her arms, and her braids lay tangled on her back. She wished for a moment she had allowed Bobbien to tie them into a knot on her head.

Both her and her opponent's bodies were slick with sweat, as well as the moisture from the incessant rain. The fire turned their skin orange. She hefted the long pole she held in her hands, brandishing it again at the man who thought to conquer her. Seren lunged, and Tulani whacked him mightily on the shins. It would leave a bad bruise there. She smiled, thinking he would curse her mightily tomorrow. Several of the elders crowed, while many females clanged the bells they held over their heads.

This was not a fair fight, but it never was. Most marriages were arranged by the eldest member of a clan. Tulani had no clan; her parents were dead, murdered by Staf Nuen's son, leaving Tulani and her grandmother alone. Bobbien would never give Tulani away. She wanted her granddaughter to choose her own mate. Seren, son of the wealthiest Quyroo clan, had decided he wanted Tulani. They had met before the Quyroo League, and Tulani had insisted on her right of a Vorged, a battle until one combatant surrendered to the will of the other. She was in the seventh hour of the battle. Seren was as strong as he was stubborn, and no matter how she managed to clobber his thick head with her pole, he lumbered on, getting up, steely determination in his starshaped eyes.

Sighing inwardly, she wondered where this desire to live here and study with Bobbien came from when her heart yearned for V'sair. The king was angry with her. She had told him she needed time. Trust between her and the Quyroos had to be forged. V'sair and his family's dreams of a peaceful planet would be nothing but a mirage in the distance if she couldn't get the support of her species. They simply would not trust her. Building their faith in her as a medicine woman as well as their greatest representative was an uphill battle fraught with enemies at every corner. Why couldn't they see her intent? She had only their best interests at heart. She could be their greatest advocate, she thought angrily.

She was still an outcast. Despite how many babies she delivered safely, bones she set to be perfect once more, or purges she created to banish illness, they treated her with mistrust and contempt. She had returned to the volcano, but Ozre also remained elusive. She tried to organize the Quyroos, show them how to use the Darracian system she knew so well to achieve equality, but they failed to follow her once the volcano ceased its eruption. Now she stayed with Bobbien, going from tree to tree, learning her birthright, studying the plants and their uses in healing. She should have slipped something into this big lummox's drink earlier, and maybe this battle would be over.

"I will have you, Tulani," he told her through gritted teeth. "I will have you or die trying."

"You know I love another," Tulani taunted back.

"Who said anything about love?"

They circled each other, their breaths ragged, chests heaving with effort. Seren bared his white teeth, his huge chest glistening with sweat. His discarded Darracian uniform lay in a damp heap on the Desa floor. He was the first to join the Darracian Army, despite his father's anger. He had more ambition than the whole Quyroo League. Only those close to the fire stay warm, he told his father. He wanted to be in the center of the blaze. He was learning things, meeting the right contacts. When Darracia changed, he expected to be front and center. Seren knew that having Tulani as his mate would ensure promotion within that army. If V'sair wanted to see the girl, he would have to keep Seren at his side. He looked at her long legs and trim figure. If anybody was going to enjoy her beautiful body, it was going to be him and him alone. She was a Quyroo and belonged with him, not a half-breed mongrel.

"You need protection, Tulani," Seren sneered. "I am here to take care of you."

Tulani laughed. "I can take care of myself!"

She charged at him, her pole slamming the side of his head, then poked him deeply in the stomach. Seren attacked her by grabbing her by the upper forearms and squeezing until her world appeared to narrow into a twirling tunnel. He banged her in the head with his forehead; stars floated before her eyes. She felt her weapon going slack in her hands and would have lost it if not for the shout that pulled her back. Bobbien was screaming for her to kick straight ahead. He was just out of her reach, so she tossed the pole, swinging back and forth, building momentum, waiting for the moment Seren's guard went down.

She went slightly slack, let her eyes roll, and watched Seren's face light up with triumph. He brought her toward him, his lips pursed for a victory kiss, when she lashed out, connecting mightily with his manhood. Seren screamed, his eyes closed with pain. Tulani jumped free, grabbed her pole, and smashed it against his head, smiling satisfactorily as the giant went facedown into the mud. Seren moaned as he rolled onto his side, his face contorted with pain mixed with hatred. Tulani put her small foot at the base of his spine, forcing him to go onto his stomach.

"I hope minKays are satisfied?" She addressed the Quyroo League respectfully, using their title with an elegant bow. They were observing from a low-hanging branch. Most were smiling, but for a large Quyroo on the end, Seren's father, Jokin.

Seren's forearms shook with weakness as he tried to push himself off the ground. Tulani slammed him hard in the shoulder, grimacing with triumph when Seren's breath escaped in a gusty exhalation. She then pushed hard, watching with a satisfied smile as Seren fell face forward onto the red dirt floor.

"You won nothing, Tulani. I will have you yet," he growled through gritted teeth.

The head of the council grunted as he slid off the tree, approached Tulani, and raised her hand to the cries of the female Quyroos. "She has proven she needs no protector."

The other older Quyroos in the league agreed with nods, save Seren's sire, Jokin, who angrily shook his red fist. "It is unseemly for a maiden to be free. Even Darracians protect the females. What is this world coming to?" he spat at his defeated son, who hung his head shamefully.

"I am not a timid maiden," Tulani shouted back, fighting the chills from the colder air on her wet skin. Water ran in rivulets down her long arms and legs to pool on the red Desa floor. "I will not be owned, not by Quyroo or Darracian. I am the high priestess."

"One trick does not a priestess make," Jokin snapped back. He hated Tulani and her prince. He still blamed them for his brother Jonis's death. Jonis had gone to the Cloud City for peace talks, against his wishes, and was the first to be beheaded by Staf Nuen, the king's traitorous brother. He trusted no one. "Make the rain stop, Tulani," he shouted. "Make it stop rotting the randam crystals." He stalked closer to her, his face drenched from the moisture, water dripping from his nose and chin. "This is punishment from the Elements, the time of rain."

A grumble of assent went through the crowd. "Yes, High Priestess, knower of all things *Dar-ra-c-ian*," he added with a sneer, "use your magic to make the suns shine again and the fruit plentiful."

It was true; since the day she had made Aqin stop its eruption, Ozre, the Element that enabled her, had disappeared. Tulani and her people had stormed the castle, helping the Darracians loyal to the king crush the rebels. The king had died that day, leaving Syos with the future of a new king with bright promise. But the improvements came slowly, if at all. The Quyroos grew impatient. Tulani attempted to rally them, teach them how to appeal to King V'sair for new laws. There were some strides in the right direction, but with each policy came unprecedented problems that overwhelmed the ill-prepared government. The Moon Council deadlocked, and not even the hopeful ideals of the young king could break the stubborn ways of both species. Fewer and fewer Quyroos showed up to Tulani's meetings. Soon, nobody came, and Tulani felt their hostility at her uselessness. Ozre never answered her pleas, leaving her to face the Quyroos afterward alone and powerless. The rain started to fall then.

At first it was a gentle mist, which grew as each day passed. Torrential downpours followed, loosening rocks, uprooting trees, creating muddy quagmires that slowed growth as well as trade. Food was becoming scarce, and if not for the supplies sent by Syos, many Quyroos would have starved. The issues were overwhelming for the immature government. Many of the newly appointed commissioners were uneducated in running these programs. There was corruption, for sure; the Quyroos were disappointed, for the promised change was not coming fast enough. The Bottom Dwellers who had abandoned their homes on the volcano in the interest of peace slowly returned, making new illegal settlements. This angered the Darracians. The king dismissed his entire Moon Council, dismayed by the violent shouting, the inability to get anything accomplished. Both V'sair and Tulani were locked in a struggle beyond their capabilities to fix.

The rain tapered off, and this silenced the crowd. They were unsure of her.

Tulani scanned the horizon, her eyes searching for a ball of familiar light, when she saw a great comet streak across the black sky. "Ozre..." she whispered, until she realized it was not the Element but simply a racing comet.

Masses of Quyroos fell to their knees, their eyes wide in their startled red faces. "It's a sign."

"It's the end of days," another moaned.

Babies cried; there were shouts of dire warnings.

"Make it do something, Priestess!" Seren called out. "Prove you have the power."

Tulani slapped his head with the stick, silencing him but not the malice she saw in his lean face.

She watched the comet rocket toward Fon Reni, wondering if V'sair saw the comet as well and felt the same sense of doom. A light rain began to fall again, hushing the crowd, and soon the ruts of the planet's surface ran with a red rain the color of blood.

IV

STAF NUEN SAT comfortably in the plush chair, smoking the pipe his host had offered him. Smoke swirled around his head, stinging his yellowed eyes, a side effect from indulging in graphen. He liked it better than krayum, the heady liquor he drank at home. It left him relaxed, did not affect his reflexes, and he could smoke himself sick, and no one would ever know. He glanced out at the reflective walls of the fortress. He was the guest of King Lothen of Planta, Reminda's younger brother.

Lothen came into the room, a squire divesting him of his armor. He threw himself into a chair opposite Staf, bare chested. A servant draped a robe over his blue, well-muscled shoulders. He adjusted the golden rings he wore on his upper arms. He had at least four on each of his biceps, curling snakes that signified great victories. There was a fortune of random crystals embedded in the metal.

Lothen shook his head like a wild stallius, freeing his shoulder-length ivory hair from a rawhide. Just like every other male here, he had shaved the sides of his head, leaving only the hair covering the top of his crown to cascade down the center of his back. For battle, they tied it in topknots on their heads. Orange tattoos covered his face in a swirling pattern. Staf knew each design was different, almost like a fingerprint. All Plantans had it done as they entered puberty. It was a mark of beauty, but Staf found it oddly distracting. Large silver hoops danced in his ears, and while the older man knew Lothen was considered handsome, he thought his feral grin off-putting. He had an oily laugh, his glittering lapis eyes darting constantly around the room. Two females prepared dishes in the background. Staf lazily rose, hand clasping the king, who bade him to reseat himself. Staf eyed the king's long, pointed fingernails with distaste.

"I see you have taken advantage of my hospitality." Lothen nodded as a servant brought him a large clear goblet. A silver fish swam in circles inside the glass. A similar goblet was brought to Staf. "You are not repulsed by our Plantan habits?" the king asked silkily.

"I have seen Reminda drink this way for many years."

They clinked their glasses, gulped rapidly, swallowed the fish whole. It squirmed down Staf's windpipe, so he belched loudly, helping to squeeze it into his stomach.

Lothen laughed loudly.

"The trick is to get it down smoothly, my lord."

"Reminda may have taught me many things, sire, but not that quaint custom."

"I barely remember my sister." Lothen frowned. "She was stolen by your brother when I was a child. We were peaceful people back then."

Staf grunted, "I don't remember you being peaceful. Your people started raiding ships. That's why my father sent us here, to negotiate."

"History is written one way and remembered another. Darracians don't negotiate; they take what they want, using their precious Fireblade as justification." Lothen laughed heartily. "Oh, don't get all high-and-mighty, my lord Nuen. How will you use your special sword now; how will you explain its extraordinary power?" He stood up. "You don't need a Fireblade to feel superior. The right warrior can use any tool to achieve what he needs. Darracians don't hold a monopoly on anything but arrogance!" Lothen shot back. "Yes," and went on, his forked tongue slipping out in his rage, "we were peaceful until your brother came to steal what didn't belong to him. We are docile no longer." He slammed his glass down on the side table.

"A tragedy." Staf covered the rim of his cup when a servant came to pour some more liquid. Lothen held his goblet up for a refill. Staf was in no position to debate with the leader. If Lothen chose to remember history his way, who was he to argue with him? Staf mentally shrugged. If he wanted to use the excuse of Darracian interference, and fail to remember that Planta served as the aggressor, he wasn't going to argue.

"You don't like it?" Lothen sneered, leaning forward, his eyes watchful.

"Much as I appreciate Your Majesty's delicious libation, I must decline. I want to be able to function tonight."

"Ha," the young king roared. "You like Naje?"

"She is entertaining."

"She is wild."

Staf dipped his head. The female had kept him busy his whole time on Planta. She was a slave, similar in build to his native Quyroos, her almond-colored skin smooth as silk. A wealth of black hair flowed around her slender form. She was a prize, captured on one of the many raids from the neighboring planet Venturian. Lothen had given him the woman soon after he arrived. He had come alone, bankrupt, deserted by his forces, the wound in his side half healed. It pained him still, and only the deep massage from Naje eased its torment. He felt a sense of peace around her that he had never known before.

She was a quiet person, watchful, understood when to talk and when he desired silence. When his dreams chased sleep, she was able to calm him as no other. Her supple arms embraced him; her hushed voice lulled him back into blissful sleep. She was not as young as he first thought, and he knew she had suffered before her capture as well as after. She ran his household on the tiny island on Planta with cool efficiency, and he knew wherever he went, Naje was going with him. She had made a home for him when he felt homeless.

After the battle for Darracia, he had escaped on his ship, only to face a mutiny when he ordered them to regroup and attack. Set adrift in a small craft, he looked for a place to land. They had expected him to die from blood loss, those sniveling cowards. His men had crawled back, asking forgiveness from his nephew, who embraced them by giving away much of his territory. Staf had lost everything—his home, his wife, his children. His oldest and youngest children had been killed. His remaining three daughters lived on Darracia still; however, he hadn't had communication with them since he escaped. For all he knew, they were dead as well. It was all gone, everything except his ambition. He considered throwing himself on V'sair's mercy but knew as long as Zayden lived, he was a marked man.

The king's bastard had followed him, from planet to planet, with a determination of a hunting jast. Time after time, Staf outwitted him, always a step ahead of the young warrior.

Staf had settled for a season on that icy cesspit called Venturian. He had accomplices there, allies who, for a price, supported him, and he stayed waiting, biding time until he could figure out where he could go. He created a new business, selling stolen items to passing criminals who stopped there. Lothen heard about him and reached out to him, offering a safe haven. Staf refused based on the long-term history of their two planets. He had made himself a base of sorts, but Zayden followed him there. The hirelings he had employed to protect him attacked his brother's bastard, leaving him for dead. Well, Staf thought ruefully, you get what you pay for—the job was ill done. Zayden lived. His bastard of a nephew disappeared into the stews of Venturian, and no amount of bribery could find him. Zayden was on Venturian, waiting for the opportunity to attack. There was not enough money on Venturian to protect him from Zayden's hatred. Staf's time there was done. He had to move on and find a new host. Staf left Venturian under the protection of Lothen, king of Planta and Reminda's younger brother.

Planta was a water planet with one small island, where the crowded population lived in a jumble of homes built in layers on top of each other. While some found the pastel colors appealing, to Staf it was a dirty place, made seedy by the lack of uniformity. It was a hodgepodge of edifices, a dilapidated, faded city. The castle was more of a fortress, built hanging over a buttress above the filthy seawater. It smelled there; the air was polluted and foul. The linens were damp with mildew, and everything had a patina of bronze, slimy mold. Much as he hated it here, he had nowhere else to go. Bina, the small moon orbiting Planta, was completely uninhabitable, mined for graphen by slaves from all over the galaxy. That left Ablas, in the far end of the solar system, which was colder than hell and about as hospitable.

He picked up the long pipe that was attached to the hanging bottle from the ceiling. A manservant dropped a blossom into the bulb, lit it with a long taper, and Staf inhaled deeply, letting the smoke envelop his airways. It was getting to the point where he needed to have the pipe in his hands all day long.

"Graphen can take over your life." Lothen sucked deeply on his own pipe, closing his eyes as the vapors filled his lungs. He released it, and Staf watched through slit lids as the smoke escaped from the gills that ran alongside the king's ribs. He had never seen Reminda's gills. They had been hidden under her clothing. He wondered briefly if V'sair had them as well, then shrugged, giving himself up to the enticing visions that followed a deep inhale.

They sat in silence, the king of the Plantans and the political rebel Staf Nuen. They were an unlikely couple, enemies their entire lives, their two governments never having found a common ground. Once, many years ago, Planta had been a peaceful planet, a land filled with fishermen and abundance. Changing circumstances had caused Reminda's father to reconsider his strategies, developing a reputation for cunning and deceit. It all started with subtle climate changes. They didn't feel it at first, but slowly resources grew tight. His home's natural commodities waning, the land and oceans became overextended. The old king started attacking convoys that traveled nearby to make up the shortages. The people became lazy, stopped creating products.

Soon, the Plantans had forgotten how to produce for themselves. It was cheaper and easier to steal. Overpopulation and pollution continued to strip Planta of its bounty. The lush gardens, famous throughout the galaxy, withered and died. The sea became a filthy swamp, the arable land reduced to one small part of an island in a sea of poison. The planet could not support the growing populations of Plantans, its resources stretched to their limits. It became known as a lawless sector of space, and many were afraid to travel there. The Plantan raiders showed little mercy and attacked without discrimination.

Talks and treaties were rebuked, and when the Darracians had approached them fifty years ago, sending a young prince to initiate peace talks, Drakko was taken prisoner. Wounded in a fray, he was nursed by the king's daughter, Reminda, who had fallen in love with him. Drakko made a daring escape and took Reminda with him. No amount of peace talks could repair the damage. Reminda's father went on a rampage, making this end of the solar system a very dangerous place. It became too risky to travel in the area. Trade routes dried up, and the neighboring cold planet of Venturian sunk into poverty. The Plantans didn't care. They raided Venturian, enslaving its inhabitants, transforming the thriving society into a dismal, barren wasteland, the most important export the slaves they plundered from the population.

Venturian was a freezing rock of a planet that had a highly successful trade from its vast and varied wildlife. Trappers first settled there, drawn by the great beasts that supplied delicious meat as well as warm furs. Rudimentary settlements grew into sizable towns. It was an uncivilized place, on the western edge of the solar system, a wild frontier, barely governed. It was a freewheeling territory, the last civilized outpost before deep space thrust a traveler into nothingness. The Plantan raids destroyed all that. Stores and businesses closed. Law enforcement was crushed by the raiders.

Vast fish farms failed, and the lively planet became a devastated way station filled with criminals who traded on violence and fear. The sprawling villages had turned into garbage heaps, filled with cheap bars and a frightened populace. Soon it was depleted to an empty shell, leaving only the rejects or infirm to live off the discarded leavings of the raiders.

Eventually, the old Plantan leader died, and his son Lothen became king. The new king didn't remember the old ways, their religion. He respected nothing. He felt confined by the restrictions of the Elements and their forced morality. Abandoning antiquated beliefs, he ordered them to rip out the Temple of the Elements. It was forbidden to mention the Sradda Doctrines. They didn't need them anymore; the Elements had abandoned them and the surrounding planets, allowing a new religion that encouraged the idea of taking what belonged to others without consequence or conscience. The ideology took root, growing in the dead soil. The cult of Geva changed the buried heart of Planta from the sweet land of peace and plenty to a place filled with hatred and greed. Dancing naked around a caldron, the Plantans paid homage to their new goddess, Geva, by sacrificing whatever she asked for. Geva was a greedy goddess, one who demanded constant loyalty, but in return, she opened the door to a new way to see things, one where Plantan needs were the only ones that mattered. She urged her followers to mow down anything in their path to prosperity. A fickle entity, she punished when ignored and rewarded the wicked path Lothen led his people.

This opened a gateway for unimaginable carnage, a total disregard for goodness. It was a new age, a dark time, a time of stealing what you wanted at the expense of your neighbor, and only the strongest survived.

Plantans didn't need the restrictions or moral code of the Elements anymore. They were raiders, pirates, and thieves under the protection of Geva's dark heart. Everything was acquired by trickery or stealth. The Plantan Navy attacked ships passing through wider and wider quadrants of the solar system. They were a fearsome and lawless group. Now, far gone with decay, Planta, too, was a dying planet. Years of abuse had taken their toll. Lothen needed a plan; his advisors warned him they had barely a year left before they must find an alternative place to live. The toxic sea was slowly poisoning the atmosphere. Venturian was out of the question; starved to a useless ball of ice, the warmth of the two suns barely touching it, it made for an unwelcome home with its year-round winter. They had to find a new home.

The two leaders sat in silence for a long while, the whisper of the servants as they moved around the room the only sound. Night gulls called. Staf opened his eyes to stare out the windows to watch them dive into the restless sea, then resurface with fish speared on their swordlike beaks. He needed to resurface. He had to shake off this lethargy to dive back into the sea and spear that little fish, his nephew. Zayden was near; Staf felt his skin tingle with anticipation. *Let him come for me,* he thought boldly. *I will take care of him and then his slimy little brother.* He needed a faster ship than the little craft he was using. A fearsome army at his command could turn the entire solar system around. He enjoyed watching Lothen plunder any Darracian convoy stupid enough to wander into their airspace. The Plantans' ruthless tactics ensured they were the power in this end of the quadrant. Not even the Elements could stop them. As much as he liked it here, felt at home, he was nothing more than a guest. Lothen was popular with his own species. There was no future for him here on this dying planet. Sooner than later, he would have to find a new place to stay. Staf longed to go home to take Darracia from his alien of a nephew. He was full-blooded Darracian and considered himself its rightful leader.

"You are thinking about your home?" Lothen asked silkily.

Staf stared at the younger man, hating him for having his own throne, even if it was withering. He wanted one too. "I am always thinking of my home."

"Reminda is a traitor to Planta."

"She is a devious insect who controlled my brother," Staf replied with venom.

"You brother was a fool. You know, Staf, I have a proposition. Time is running out for me here. Planta cannot continue to sustain us for much longer. I need to find a new place for my people."

"What about Venturian?" Staf growled, his blood-shot eyes narrow.

Lothen glanced up and motioned for all his servants to leave the room. Staf's sullen Venturian slave left with a lingering glare at her master, who laughed at her rebelliousness.

"She is hot-tempered, that one." Lothen poured another drink.

"She is a challenge; it pleases me." Staf sucked on the pipe, his breath hitching on the inhalation. The room took on a pink, hazy glow, and Lothen wavered in the smoke. "Together we could use my fleet to attack Darracia." "Darracia?" Staf sat up, intrigued.

"Yes, it would be perfect. My army is unstoppable. We are seasoned soldiers when it comes to invasion. We have practiced on Venturian for years."

"Darracians are not Venturians. They will fight and may defeat you," Staf stated.

Lothen shrugged. "Think you your nephew will lead the Darracians against me? I have the power of Geva here!" Lothen laughed as he pointed to his hair-less blue chest.

"We are known to be excellent warriors." Staf blew pale smoke through his nose, feeling the sting.

"Darracian, Plantan, what difference does it make? I need a new home, and so do you, my friend."

"There can be only one leader," Staf stated, his eyes glittering with purpose. He sat up straighter, the ache in his side gone.

"My people will not answer to you." Lothen watched the spray swirl above the filthy ocean. "You need me." He paused as if an idea had just come to him. "I have an idea. Your heir is dead. Make me your successor, and I will aid you with my armies. We will get rid of the Darracian ruling class, supplant it with a new one, loyal to you. I will have my men marry their daughters, take their property. What have your Elements ever done for you, given you false hope with your fire sword? We shall create a new world order. A world order loyal to Geva."

"A world order loyal to you." Staf stood, slightly unsteadily. "I do not know this…this Geva. I don't know of its power. What of the Elements? They will not stand for it. Ozre chose his side."

"They will be loyal to whom I direct them to be. They are not Darracians. As for Ozre, surely you don't believe in fairy tales?"

"You believe in Geva? Is it not a fairy tale too?"

"She. Geva, goddess of power. Someday, when you are ready, I will show you Geva, and you will feel the might of her will."

Staf stood up, weaving, pausing to consider how to say what he felt. "I don't see her might on this dying planet. Perhaps she will change her doctrine when you need her the most?"

Lothen jumped up to angrily pace the room. "You believed in your Fireblade…Can you say for sure, without a doubt, that the Elements really exist? Have you faced them?" he demanded.

Staf considered the question, choosing his words carefully. "For years we were taught to practice our skills until the night we became one with the Fireblade."

"We do not have a Fireblade. Plantans don't need them."

Staf acknowledged this with a nod. "A Darracian male is taught, well, was taught, that our strength is enhanced by the will of the Fireblade, and only because of our superiority, we are able to maintain the balance of power."

"You believe that, my lord. We don't have a Fireblade, yet we have the totality of power. Perhaps Geva does not believe in toys but in the power of real men."

Staf closed his eyes in thought. "V'sair should not have been able to harness the power." He opened his eyes and realized he was talking to another blood relative of his nephew. "Yet he surprised us all with great skill. It is said he looked into his own heart and found the strength to command the Fireblade."

"Strength is developed, not given by imagined beings."

"The Elements are real."

"It is your belief. The Elements are not real here on Planta; the only thing that matters is me and what I think."

"And what do you think, Your Majesty?"

"I think that the combined forces of Staf Nuen and a Plantan Army can teach young V'sair that merely closing one's eyes and wishing for power is a dream."

"Then let it be his nightmare." Staf puffed on his pipe. "Your men will be loyal to you in a fight for a distant planet?"

"And to you as well, my liege."

"You would call me your liege?" Staf pressed his face close to Lothen, their breaths intermingling, the fumes of Lothen's drink making Staf dizzy.

"I would call you Father if you made me your heir…" Lothen whispered. "Do it, Staf. Do it," he wheedled. "Why stop at Darracia? We can rule the solar system. With Darracian riches, Quyroo and Venturian slaves, by Geva's heart, we can control the entire galaxy."

Staf wheeled away, light-headed. It was the answer to

his dreams. Plantan might, with his leadership—V'sair wouldn't stand a chance. He would crush him. Staf made a fist and pressed it against the window, trying hard to conceal his growing excitement. The universe was within his grasp.

"What of the Elements? They will stop us."

"If they are real, then Geva will destroy them," Lothen told him passionately.

"Perhaps," Staf told him impatiently, wondering if indeed the Elements were nothing more than a chimera, as Lothen indicated. "Maybe Geva is not real as well?"

"Give me time to prove she is not only real but more powerful than anything in this universe."

Staf slid back into the comfort of the chair, picking up the pipe once more. He clicked the pipe against his teeth, deep in thought. "You would let me do what I wanted?"

"That is usually what a vassal does with his liege."

"Why? Here you are king, leader of many people. Why would you subjugate yourself to me?"

"You know how they think. If we work together, I won't have to be confined to this part of the system. Planta is withering." Lothen stood up. "We've exhausted our food supply; the fuel is gone from the ocean. We are running out of options."

"Why does not your Geva act to save you and your planet?"

"Perhaps her plan was to unite us, my lord Nuen. Who knows the mysteries of a goddess?"

"You would not be king there for a long time."

"I am known for my patience." Lothen laughed, his

forked tongue visible. "I am prepared to do this with or without you."

"Yes?" Staf raised his dark brow.

"I have an ally."

"Who?" Staf demanded. "Who did you find to betray Darracia and why?"

"Someone very close to the throne, to your nephew, the king." Lothen's voice was soft and menacing. "I have spies planted there, both Quyroo as well as Darracian."

"Why would two opposing forces help you?" Staf asked.

"When you promise them their heart's desire, you have no need to search for allies."

"In the same way you promise me?" Staf asked quietly.

"Surely it is not the same, my lord Nuen. We are cut from the same cloth. I could never betray you," Lothen said with a slick smile. He slapped Staf on the back and laughed. "The weather is changing here. I don't know how long this planet will survive. I can be your grand mestor." He called loudly for the servants to return with fresh goblets. "Let's drink on it."

A new libation was brought over, this time with a bloodred fish swimming furiously in it. Staf looked at the creature and realized it had human head, chest, and arms but a fishlike tail. He could hear the sound of its screams.

"The Talis. They live deep in our oceans and are quite a nuisance. A sacrifice on the altar of your success."

A keening wail rent the air behind him, and the king spun, sloshing his drink.

A female servant covered her eyes as she screamed,

pointing to the night sky. "An omen, sire, surely 'tis the end of the world."

The king and Staf edged close to the window, spying a careening comet spinning wildly across the vast sky, its reflection lighting the waves.

"A portent of doom?" Lothen watched the jagged trail of the comet streaking across the horizon.

"A sign of change. Change for the better." Staf held up his glass, laughing at the horror on the creature's face as he downed his drink in one giant gulp. He felt the being slide down his gullet as he smacked his lips with appreciation.

"To Geva!"

"To our partnership, with Geva at the spearhead!" the king agreed.

"Death to all who defy us." Staf watched with fascination as the king devoured the helpless sea creature.

V

ZAYDEN BENT OVER the chassis of his ship and blew gently against the sand that layered the engine. The ship had been made especially for him, the curved chassis white with green and blue racing stripes. It was a sweet goer with plenty of muscle that got him in more than a little trouble with its speed. Wiping his greasy hands on a torn piece of material, he jumped into the bucket seat and tried to turn over the turbo. He heard the squeal and grind of the sand against his gears and winced as it stalled once again. Cursing, he swung out of his cockpit and searched the sky angrily. He had waited too long. His engine was pitted with rust, his gears dried, the thrusters clogged with the ever-present sand that covered the beaches where he had landed. He hadn't cared back then. It had only been a week, and he was careless. He had landed here so he could regroup, think of how he was going to proceed.

He had Denita with him, and he needed to figure out what to do with her. Going back to Venturian was out of the question. Together, they had watched her home burn. Though she had marked him with a tattoo, she was the one who was really marked. By helping him, she had given up any chance of being safe there, and while she thought herself to be tough, he refused to leave her to their brutality. He would take her home; Reminda would know what to do with her. Then he would go after Staf and kill him. He could never rest until the deed was done and both his father and Hilde were avenged.

It had been a long journey so far, and the older man eluded him everywhere. He had followed Staf to Venturian, an icy shit hole in the back end of the solar system, to wander the shadowy brothels and graphen dens where some went in but never came out. Venturian was a tough place to be asking questions. The population was as unhelpful as they were unfriendly. He combed the gritty stores and dens, asking too many questions. He drew all the wrong attention, and it didn't take long before he knew he was being tailed. He dodged in and out of the freezing doorways, trying to lose his pursuers, but they remained hot on his trail. It had swelled to a group, and he realized he was vastly outnumbered. He needed to get back to the harbor, to the safety of his ship. He withdrew his pistol, ducking in and out of the winding streets, and saw they were coming from two different directions. He was in big trouble. He feinted left, but ran to the right into a deserted alleyway, panicking when he realized this one was a dead end. Doors slammed shut; it seemed the citizens of Venturian had a laissez-faire attitude toward crime, especially when it wasn't happening to them. They were on him in an instant, the pistol snatched from his hands, but not before he got off a shot and heard a howl of pain. A two-by-four hit him in the stomach, followed by someone kicking his head, hard, really hard. Before his eyes rolled backward, he heard a female shout and the sizzle of another gun. Something the size of a Darracian hit the back of his head, and then nothing until he woke in a run-down room in the rear of a graphen den.

He ached everywhere, his skull and ribs most of all. Sounds were muffled, and he saw everything in a distorted lens. He knew there was a woman taking care of him with the efficiency of a competent nurse, but everything else moved in slow motion. Smoke filled his head, and he burned with fever. Cool hands had soothed him. He had a faint memory of searing pain in his shoulder coupled with whispered words that he was marked. He woke with a throat so dry it hurt to swallow. Iron bands constricted his rib cage. His head ached with the intensity of a thousand banging drums. Soft fingers brushed his hair back, and a wavering vision of a beautiful, black-haired, sloe-eyed female with skin the color of caramel appeared in his line of sight. She held his head up for a drink, a smile on her wide carmine-colored mouth.

"Slowly, Warrior." She pulled the cup away from

his dehydrated lips. She had a deep voice that reminded Zayden of liquid mercury, both soft and smoky.

"Where am I?" The words came out in a croak. "This is my den."

Zayden attempted to rise.

"Stay still. You are safe, for now."

His shoulder ached as though acid had drenched it. He raised an unsteady hand to touch it, and she caught it within her own.

"Don't touch it."

"What...was I shot?"

"By me." She smiled down at him. "My needle. I have branded you." She ran her hands down his gray, pebbled chest possessively. "I saved you, and you belong to me."

"I don't think so." Zayden groaned from his gut as he rose, attempting to get off the pallet. "What is your name?"

"Denita." She turned her back and went to her cooking fire to fill a plate from a bubbling pot. "You will be hungry, I am thinking. Darracians are meat eaters, yes?" She ladled an overfilled spoon into a crude bowl, and Zayden's stomach growled loudly in the tiny room.

Sick as he was, he still noticed her tight-fitting black jumpsuit that hugged every curve. She wore high black boots that ended at the middle of her long thighs. She had a great pair of legs; Zayden eyed them with admiration. Though he wasn't interested, he still enjoyed looking at an attractive woman, and she was attractive. They were in close quarters, clearly in the rear of a noisy graphen den. It was dingy, a beaded curtain the only privacy from the patrons in the next room. Drafts blew through the chinks in the walls; his skin contracted with cold. He shivered involuntarily, and Denita threw a wrap around his wide shoulders, caressing him possessively until he shook her off. Denita had a pallet, two mismatched chairs, and a table that listed with a broken leg. Zayden walked unsteadily to the table and sat down heavily on the chair, his head feeling miles above his body. The girl dropped the bowl before him. Zayden pushed his snarled hair from his face. Denita stood behind him, stroking his head lovingly.

"Stop that." He slapped at her weakly.

"You didn't mind last night," she told him seductively, taking a brush and beginning to comb through his tangled locks. "Oh, it is a mess. I am going to braid it."

He felt her tugging on his scalp and moved his head away.

She tapped him on the shoulder with the brush. "Don't make me hurt you. Otherwise I'll just cut all your hair off. You'll feel better after you eat. You've been out of it for a couple of days."

Zayden knew the days were longer than on his native Darracia, this planet being so far from the suns.

"How many?" His voice was a rusty scrape.

She looked at him with a question in her eyes, which he noticed were a rich dark-brown framed by two dense rows of mink-colored lashes.

"Days, how many days have I been here?"

She shrugged. "Oh, I found you four days ago. You

were trying to attack a group of robbers. One slightly broken Darracian against fifteen thugs. No matter how talented you are, the odds were not in your favor."

"Why did you help me?" Zayden shoveled a spoonful of potted meat into his mouth. It was delicious, and he was ravenous.

Denita observed him with a possessive smile. She filled a glass with a white liquid and put it on the table. "Drink it. It will help."

Zayden took a gulp and recoiled at the overly sweet taste.

"It is good for you."

"I don't want it." He pushed it away, slightly nauseated.

"But you will drink it." Denita pushed it back and finished, "My warrior."

"Stop saying that. I'm not your warrior." He touched his cheek, wincing at its tenderness. His hand moved up, and he realized his patch was missing. "Where is it?" he demanded.

"You don't need it with me. I have seen far more of you than that." Denita laughed as she threw his frayed patch onto the table.

Zayden hastily put it on, feeling his shoulder pull. Looking down, he saw a strange blue circle within a black circle covering most of his shoulder. He touched it lightly.

"It tells everyone you are mine. I saved you, and now you belong to me."

"I belong to no one."

"You owe me, Darracian. A life for a life." She swiftly rolled her sleeve up, showing him a white bandage.

Deftly she removed it, revealing a long gash. "This is the price I paid. We are hardly even." Turning, she left him to eat alone. He heard her commanding voice rapping out orders in the next room.

Suddenly weary, he staggered to the lumpy cot, and his head hit the spare pillow to fall deeply into a healing sleep.

He awoke to silence, the rich time before the suns rose, when dew graced the ground, coating the grass like sugarspun crystals, untouched by the filthy rabble inhabiting the planet. Zayden flexed his legs, feeling stronger than he had, and rolled to his feet. The room was empty, the wind barely moving the ragged curtains. He looked around, spied his pistol on the table, rolled upward to snatch it, and put it in the back of his pants. He staggered up, finding the place he needed, his body's urges making themselves known.

"Ah, so you've finally passed water. Is it still bloody?"

Zayden felt his face heat up. "It's no business of yours." He pushed himself into the small kitchen, weaving just a bit.

"Sit down, you big lunk. You are going to ruin all my handiwork." She plunked another bowl of something steaming onto the crude table. "Was me that fought off those hired baboons and sewed up your cuts. Around here that deserves a bit of gratitude. I own you, Warrior."

Zayden laughed. "You can't own a dead man. I died a year ago."

"You mean Hilde?"

Zayden stalked to her and grabbed her arm, surprised

by the strength in her corded muscles. "How do you know about Hilde?" he demanded, his teeth bared.

"Settle down before you fall down. You talked is all." She shrugged out of his grip as he sat heavily onto the chair. "She's dead. I'm not. So accept your new reality."

"By the great Sradda, you will not tell me what to do!" Zayden shouted, but the fight was leaving him.

"There are no Elements here, Warrior. They left us to the Plantans years ago. On Venturian, we only have our wits, and this." She reached down and held up a Fireblade in her strong hand.

"Where did you get that?"

"I took it off a dead man. The one who had taken it from you." She threw it to him, and he deftly caught it. "Now you will teach me how to use the Fireblade."

Zayden shook his head. "I cannot teach you. It has no power." He tucked it into the loop of his pants.

"It does so…"

Zayden dropped his spoon, his amber eye narrowed. "How could you know?"

"I'll show you." Denita held out a calloused hand.

"When you hold it with both hands…"

"You had a flame?" Zayden asked quietly.

"Well, it was weak, but I am sure if you showed me how to--"

"What color was it?" Zayden demanded.

"What difference does it make? Relax, Warrior, I think it was a light blue; I admit it was weak."

"Don't touch it. It's forbidden. Don't ever touch it ever again." Zayden stared at her hard. She was younger than he first thought, but years of living in this hellhole had hardened her. He thought her to be a few years younger than he. "Why do you want to learn?" The room became so still, the air seemed to solidify.

Denita spoke almost in a whisper. "The Plantans have something of mine, and I have to get it back."

"What?"

"None of your business."

"Fine…Thanks for all you've done." He picked his jacket off the back of a chair, sliding his arm painfully into it.

"You can't leave. You owe me."

"Give me your address, and I'll have my people send you something."

"Oh, very funny, Your Highness."

Zayden turned and grabbed her wrist, his knuckles white. "What do you mean by that?" he asked, a fine white line rimming his lips.

"Nothing." Denita pulled away, her mouth thin with hatred. "You're hurting me. I don't want your money. I want your help."

Zayden shrugged. "I left my ship at the harbor. It's probably on its way to Pagil 7 in a million little pieces. Besides, I don't know Planta or its terrain. I don't even know what you're so hot to find. You don't even know me."

"I know enough. When you walk around Venturian asking questions, everybody is aware of you. Just get me to Planta, and I'll do the rest, Zayden."

"How do you know my name?" he demanded.

"Everybody on Venturian knows your name. They

also know that I am the only one willing to help you. If not for me, you'd be nothing but fertilizer."

"Whatever." Zayden shrugged. "I will not help you. I am looking for Staf Nuen."

"So am I," Denita told him with finality.

Zayden's knees shook, so he sat down, abashed at his weakness. "Not gonna happen, sweetheart."

"We'll see about that, *sweetheart*," Denita called back nastily as she left the room and their debate.

Zayden's lips split into a grin in spite of himself. She was as ornery as the horned toads of Fon Reni, but he had to admit she had a great little…He stopped to wonder how she had gotten the flame to turn blue.

The attack came the next morning without warning. Plantan raids were ruthless, as well as indiscriminate. The cries of the locals mixed with the blades of the invaders. He heard Denita's defiant voice fill the small den.

"He's not here, I tell you." A scabbard screamed as a blade was raised. Zayden grabbed his Fireblade from the floor next to his cot, feeling the flame of it come to life. He hadn't touched it as a weapon for almost a year but instinctively reached for it when he heard Denita's arguing. Looking at it with loathing, he looped it in his pants and took out his pistol. Hiding behind the beads, he saw Denita surrounded; a small nick in her neck dripped red with blood. His head heated up with rage, his amber eye glazed with hate.

"Even if he was here, I wouldn't let you have him!" she shouted.

A great sword arc upward, Zayden cursed loudly,

bursting through the curtain, firing off two rapid rounds, taking out both the man holding a knife to Denita's throat, and the other one by the door. Denita withdrew a small, wickedlooking blade from a sheath attached to the boot by her calf and gut stabbed the last raider.

"Why did you do that! I was fine without your help!" Denita spun on him.

"Yeah…I can see just how fine." He touched the droplet of blood dripping down her long neck.

She recoiled, her back ramrod straight, looking like a proper little soldier. "You've ruined everything. I had it under control."

"A regular general," Zayden said sarcastically.

Denita touched her neck, cursing at the pain. "We have to get out of here," she said urgently. "There'll be more coming now."

Zayden ripped a piece of his shirt and with an intimate gesture dabbed her neck. She pulled away, and Zayden grabbed her arm, forcing her to bare her neck. Their eyes locked. Her skin was soft, and he touched a rough knuckle to the vulnerable underside of her chin. She moved her face higher. It almost felt like an offer, he thought. She moistened her lips, her lovely lashed eyes wide in her small face. They stared at each other in silence, until she hissed in pain.

Zayden muttered softly, "Well, I have nowhere to go." "Your ship," she told him, her lips inches from his own.

Zayden looked down at her. Time seemed frozen, when he suddenly threw the scrap of cloth in a corner, angry at himself for caring. Feelings were for others, not him.

"My ship is gone and of no use," he said flatly.

"No, no, it is safe. It was missing a binding plug and a masen board. I had them replaced." She grabbed his hand. They stopped at the door; the icy streets were striated with blood. Still warm, it made a miasma of steam and filled the air with an iron-like odor. Venturians were murdered as they stood; screams pierced the air. Smoke swirled around them, obliterating the shabby storefronts. Zayden coughed, his ribs protesting mightily. Fires dotted the street where Plantans had thrown lit torches onto the wooden roofs.

Zayden hung on the door, breathless, his head wound weeping, falling to his knees in the icy slush. *Where are the Elements now?* he demanded. How could they stand by and watch beings mowed down, letting them be plundered by tribes that knew no mercy?

"Move, Warrior!" Denita placed a shoulder under his arm. "This way."

He turned to watch her home go up in a blaze, falling when an explosion rent the air. Her home went up in a fireball, raining debris over their heads. Ducking his aching head, he watched burnt pieces of flesh splatter the icy, rutted lanes.

"The graphen." Denita smiled, her face lit up by the flames. "It's highly unstable. I hope those bastards were still inside."

He pointed to smoking flesh. "Looks like your wishes came true."

"If only…" she replied harshly.

"Well, this bastard is ready to go," Zayden told her, holding her by the elbow. "Which way, Denita?"

"Follow me."

They sprinted through the back alley, slipping in the freezing mud. Zayden panted as they weaved between the burning buildings. All around him, he could hear cries for mercy, and the sounds of rampage. The Plantans pushed in doorways, carrying whatever they could on their backs, including the young women of the colony. Zayden gripped his sidearm, turning to enter the fray, when he felt Denita tug his arm.

"This is not your fight."

"It seldom is," Zayden responded. "They are carrion."

"They have my sister. I need you," Denita implored him.

He looked at the carnage. His amber eye narrowed as he turned to help the victims.

"You won't make a difference here! They do this all the time. Look, do you want me to beg?" she demanded. They stood frozen, eyes locked, and Zayden swore he saw all the way to her soul. It was just as bleak as his own.

Denita pushed him into a small building. Zayden gasped when he recognized a familiar outline underneath a tarpaulin. Sweat glistened off her almond-colored skin.

"Warrior, help me," she urged him.

With his good arm, Zayden pulled the heavy material off the dulled surface of his ship, his ribs screaming in protest.

"You didn't wax it?"

"Idiot. Get us out of here."

"Hop in."

He climbed up, hauling himself in as the door burst open, revealing a group of Plantan warriors with bloodlust in their eyes, swords and spears held high. Punching the thrusters, he gave a satisfied grin when they roared to life, and without regard for his sore shoulder, he shoved it to the maximum level, praying to all the Elements that he wouldn't stall.

A huge Plantan jumped onto his wing, and Zayden cried out to Denita, "Buckle up, buttercup!"

The engines squealed with power, and he felt the giddiness that always preceded the burst of speed his ship was capable of. They shot out of the building with dizzying speed, the warrior peeled off by the force of gravity.

His ship picked up momentum as it left the embattled planet but did not escape notice of a Plantan hunting party. His left arm almost useless, Zayden swerved his ship toward the blazing suns, hoping his maneuver would blind his pursuers. He felt the jolt as one of the heat seekers grazed the wing of his small ship, making it go into a wild spin. Denita pounded on the glass that separated their compartments with her fists.

"Not now, sweetheart," he yelled sarcastically, "I'm sort of busy!" Gritting his teeth, he grabbed the wheel, sparks of pain flashing behind his eyes from his busted ribs. His hand went numb, but he held on, pressing for as much power to go to his tiny engines. He loved his ship. It had been a gift from his father for his captaincy. It was compact and the fastest on Darracia. The engine screamed in the void of space, zipping under the startled pirates to escape into the darkness beyond the atmosphere.

"You okay there, Denita?" No answer.

"Denita?" He painfully shifted in his seat and saw a fine line of blood from a hairline cut. "Shit."

He needed a place to think. He needed to heal his wounds. He turned his ship and headed to Fon Reni.

♦

The brush swayed, and Denita stood in her torn black jumpsuit proudly holding a dead pozin in her hand. It had been a dicey few hours after he landed, according to him, crashed as far as she was concerned. Denita suffered a concussion; she had never belted herself in, as there had not been time. Her head connected hard with the dashboard, and she missed the entirety of their daring escape. After they landed, Zayden pulled her from the ship painfully, stripped out of his shirt, and doused it with cold seawater to place on her head. It took a few hours, but she returned to him, angrily cursing that he didn't land on Planta.

"Where is this place?" she spit, mobile once again.

"Fon Reni."

"Fon Reni? Fon Reni!" she shouted. "You take me to a resort when we can avenge my family!" She paced the indigo beach shakily. "Take me to Planta, now!"

"No can do, General." Zayden didn't look up from the small fire he was building. "I would remove the boots before you burn your feet through them. The sand doesn't react well to the material of your soles," he explained calmly.

"Don't tell me what to do, and don't call me general," she grumbled.

They barely talked for the rest of the day. Denita had taken herself off to explore the dense forest of swaying palms, and he had removed his shoes and rolled up his pants to enjoy the gleam of the suns bouncing off the golden ocean. "She's back." He smirked hearing her stomping through the brush madder than a wet gresh.

She eyed the pile of discarded crab. "You ate already," she accused him with disgust, laying her catch beside the fire. She stared at the ribbed muscles of his chest, gleaming in the firelight. He had the rough, pebbled skin of the Darracians; she saw that his chest was a lighter gray than the rest of him, with big purple bruises covering half his torso. She knew he was still in considerable pain. His shoulders gleamed in the firelight. The shadows played off the sculpted angles of his lean face.

"Didn't you hear the dinner bell?" Zayden looked up innocently. "You snooze, you lose."

"I wasn't sleeping. Unlike some, I was checking this place out for a way to get off. And I trapped a pozin as well." She kicked it toward him with the toe of her boot.

Zayden held up his index finger. "One, we are alone. My family owns the rights to Fon Reni, and no one can come here without permission. Two"—he touched the next finger—"pozin are foul, nasty rodents that have a scent sac that makes them inedible."

"You could have left me some crabs. Who is your family?"

Zayden ignored her question and simply said, "Look in the basket." He pointed to the container with a small wave of dismissal.

Denita walked over to him and leaned against the side of his ship. "We go to Planta?" she asked hopefully.

"No. We are going home."

"I don't have a home."

"But I do."

VI

TULANI RACED THROUGH the treetops, her arms grabbing one branch after another effortlessly. Her upper torso had developed, and she wasn't the soft cloud dweller anymore. She grabbed the slippery vines with her calloused hands, but still worried she would slide down and find herself on the wet Desa floor if she wasn't careful.

"Wait up, you keewalla!" Bobbien called from behind her.

She was faster than her grandmother and smiled, her white teeth gleaming in the darkness. Her hair bounced against her back, her braids thick and numerous. "Faster, Greanam. I want to get out of here. It's pouring."

It had started raining in the last moon phase and never stopped. It was a steady downpour; the randam crystals rotted on the bark. Flowers failed to bloom, and fruits were scarce. This was unprecedented, and the Quyroos complained but failed to see the impending disaster. Food stores were running low. Even the wysbies had disappeared, their wings too fragile to fly in the downpours.

She was headed for Aqin, their home. They had moved into the vast chambers to be closer to Ozre. Tulani had so much to learn, but try as she might, the Element was elusive. Bobbien used the time to teach her about the herbs and medicines of the forest, but Tulani was miserable. She missed V'sair and felt she could not return until she understood her role in this world. No longer a servant, not quite a healer, a half-fast high priestess, she was floundering in her own insecurities. She needed to make a connection to her people. She knew her role was to serve as conduit to the king, but she felt as removed from them as she did when she lived in Syos, the city of the clouds.

"Just go to V'sair if you are unhappy here," Bobbien told her, clearly out of patience for her lovesick sighs. "I am tired of seeing Seren's nasty face stalking you."

The big Quyroo hadn't given up and frequently could be found just watching their home. She would often catch a glimpse of him hiding in the treetops, his narrowed eyes cold.

"I am not afraid of that one." She dismissed Seren with a disinterested shrug. "I can't leave, Greanam. V'sair wants me as his queen. I don't want to be an ornament; I want to make a difference. I fear I know nothing. I need to be able to help. I want to make a difference."

"Yes, I do agree, child. Time—you need time to learn to use the Elements to achieve greatness, I think. Yes, you do."

"But the Quyroos still don't accept me."

"They are leery of you, they are," Bobbien said with a sage nod. "Don't trust you, don't trust nobody, the Quyroos. You understand why, don't you?"

Tulani thrust out her lower lip. "It's all so exhausting. We are caught in this terrible limbo. V'sair strives to make peace; Darracians act superior; the Quyroos don't trust them." She plopped down next to her grandmother. "Some mountains are too hard to climb."

"Defeatist talk!" Bobbien yelled at her, her red face turning an unbecoming shade of magenta. "Remember you not Ozre telling you to look inside your heart?"

"I have, and all I see is love for V'sair."

"Then go and live only for your love!" Bobbien got up to angrily ready their next meal. She threw ingredients around like a mad chef, and Tulani bit back a smile. "Whiney, whiney," said her grandmother. "You think everything should come in a snap?" She held up her hand and snapped her long fingers impatiently. "You have just learned of our healing ways, crammed years of training into mere months. If you want to be accepted by your people, you have to become one of them."

"I am Quyroo," Tulani told her defensively.

"Physically, yes, but up here"—she pointed to her temple—"I think not. Do not blame others for your lack of success. Search your mind to see what more you can do."

"Did Ozre tell you that?"

"He didn't have to," Bobbien replied curtly, then turned back to pound some forest edibles into a pulp.

So they settled in the caves, gathering the roots, making potions. Tulani studied the Quyroos and slowly began to see their way of thinking. Every night she threw herself onto the cold stone floor, called for Ozre, but heard nothing. "Why have you deserted me, Ozre," she cried out. "I need your guidance."

The echoes of her pleas were her only response.

VII

"HIGHNESS, WE MUST schedule the coronation," General Swart stated from his seat on the Orbitus Chamber, a group that met daily with the king.

"I am still in mourning, General. It is out of the question," V'sair answered absently, his gaze on the condensation coating the wall of windows. "It's filthy out there today," he added to no one in particular.

"A strange occurrence, for sure." Brault, the chanter, added with his querulous voice. "The weather is strange. We have not seen Rast or Nost for months. Rain, rain, rain, it's making the whole Desa run red like blood."

"Enough, Chanter Brault," V'sair said curtly. He didn't like the man. He had been appointed to the head of the Temple of the Elements, and V'sair hadn't warmed to him. It had been a fair appointment; he was chosen by a group of lesser chanters. Due to his seniority, it was a given that he should lead the temple. Short and dumpy, he had a long, thin nose and beady eyes that seemed too close together.

Chanters shaved their heads when they took their religious orders in order to be able to hear the Elements better. He wore the maroon robes of high office, with a golden breastplate signifying he was the most high warrior for the Elements. V'sair thought him an ugly little man, whose wrinkled and faded skin gave him the appearance of something that lived underground to tunnel in the soil. He was small-minded, hated the Quyroos, and basically made life in the Orbitus Chamber very difficult for V'sair.

But it was true—the weather had changed. It was a few degrees colder, and they'd had unexplained record rainfalls. V'sair had appointed a committee to study the problem. He had yet to hear anything from them.

V'sair fiddled with a pen. "Enough about the weather." He glanced up at a map of the Desa that hung suspended in midair. He motioned with his hands, and the images changed, from topical, to bird's-eye, to frontal. V'sair studied the screens, searching every face for the familiar one so dear to him. He saw panicked people, filthy and shocked, their homes destroyed. "How many people were hurt?" There had been a major mudslide with many casualties. V'sair wanted to organize relief efforts.

"The coronation, sire," Swart appealed.

"Will wait. What happened on the hills of Aqin?"

"It's all this rain. The Bottom Dwellers have been

flooded out of the illegal settlements. We have set up refugee camps in the Plains of Dawid."

"How do you expect me to think about things like coronations when my people suffer?" V'sair rounded on General Swart.

"How can you call them your people when you haven't been properly crowned!" Swart stood angrily. "Perhaps all this is a sign from the Elements."

"What kind of sign?" V'sair's back went rigid as he inquired quietly.

"I meant nothing, Your Highness. I am only looking for the good of the monarchy." Swart leaned closer to V'sair.

"Walk with me, sire."

V'sair stood and strolled the chamber next to his grand mestor, their footsteps echoing off the slick floor.

The general waited until they had passed a distance to give them privacy. "I have information." "Yes?" V'sair looked at him intently.

"The interrogations of the assassins have been troubling." Swart frowned.

"What have you discovered?"

Swart looked around the room, his eyes darting to every dark corner. "I am taking every precaution for your safety. But, sire, I am not happy…I feel that we are missing something."

"What, General? You did an excellent job. You intercepted them before anything happened." V'sair placed his hand on the general's stooped shoulders. "I know I am a sore trial to you, my lord general, but, like my father before me, I trust you with my life."

"Thank you, Your Majesty."

"You used to call me V'sair."

"I am worried, my…V'sair. Although they have talked, I suspect they know someone close to you is involved. I am nervous."

V'sair shrugged his shoulders. "I feel secure in your hands. But please, General, make sure my mother is safe."

"I have doubled the guards on you both."

V'sair placed a trusting hand on his shoulder. "I knew I could depend on you."

"But, sire, I would feel better if we had the coronation. It would give you legitimacy as the king. Besides, all the people love the pageantry."

"Well then use funds for all this pageantry to get supplies to the ones suffering down there." He pointed a finger to the grayness outside. He watched the general shake his head and go back to the large stone conference table where the rest of his council argued. Walking slowly to the window, he was oblivious to the discussions taking place behind him. He glanced through the gloom, wondering if Tulani was safe, warm, dry, and safe.

He didn't want to be crowned. It felt so final, as though his father was really gone. He stared at his reflection in the window, and the room receded as mist hovered, changing shapes over his head. It spangled the air, filling it with the smell of ozone, and his hair went static, rising off his scalp. All sound receded as he watched the image of his father materialize in the window. The face floated, becoming fuzzy, indistinct. It became more clear as a familiar body took shape next to V'sair. The reflection smiled sweetly, the eyes lit with incandescence. Drakko was healthy and whole, taller than V'sair. The boy rubbed his eyes, afraid to blink lest the apparition disappear. He glanced to his advisors, noting them locked in heated comments, then looked back at the specter. A smile spread across his father's generous mouth. He nodded to his son, and V'sair felt tears sting behind his eyes. Pressure landed on the young man's shoulders; V'sair touched the spot, knowing without a doubt his father had just squeezed him affectionately. Strong hands reached up, lifting the crown from his own dark head to hold it over V'sair's blond one. The jewels sparkled with the reflection of the waning light, and he watched in wonder as his father placed it on his head. Though he knew nothing graced his pate, he felt the crown's heavy weight resting there. Their eyes met to make a peaceful communion. Drakko pointed back to the council and shook his head with sorrow, letting V'sair know he was not happy with the discord. He watched those eyes rest on each of the Orbitus representatives, and while he frowned, V'sair couldn't read his father's thoughts. Then the lips moved with a soft whisper, and V'sair distinctly heard his father say, "Reminda." The shimmering reflection winked, dissolving into nothing.

V'sair touched his head, then the corner of his eye, wiping a crystal tear that had gathered there. Beyond speech, he cleared his throat noisily. Turning slowly, he looked at his councilors arguing over petty nonsense. He tried to figure out what his father was trying to tell him, but the whole thing was a muddle, from the councilors to the wet planet surface. Great Sradda, he wished Zayden were here to help him. He had to take command; the apparition, his father, had indicated it. Taking a deep breath, V'sair made a decision.

"General, arrange for my coronation for the first moon phase. We will do it in the temple. I want representatives from the Quyroos equally present. In fact, I will have one from the Quyroo League crown me."

"Out of the question!" Brault fumed.

"That's my job.

That is our custom!"

"We will circumvent the custom." V'sair turned his back. "That is all for today. Send in my mother."

Swart grumbled as he stuffed his notes into a briefcase. "Now he wants the coronation and within weeks. How am I supposed to get this done so quickly?"

Chanter Brault nodded, his face gray with indignation, and whispered, "I knew nothing good would come from the Plantan influence. A Quyroo crown him, indeed!" They walked out of the room, Brault tense with anger.

Reminda floated in, her face serene. "You asked for me?"

V'sair took her hand and kissed it. "Yes, Mo'mo. I have decided to go ahead with the coronation. You must find Tulani. I want her by my side."

"I will do my best, sire." She smiled and bowed her head.

VIII

V'SAIR STALKED TO the temple, walking purpose-fully down the long aisle to come close to the altar. It was a high-ceilinged room, the walls made of clear quartz, polished to a sparkling shine. Fossils of tiny prehistoric insects were frozen in the depths of the rock walls, testifying to both its age and majesty. It was a cool room, and when filled with Darracians, the walls reflected the array of colors adorning its inhabitants. Today it was empty, so the sleek ice-looking walls mirrored his bleak mood.

The altar stood before him on a high platform, completely carved from clear, solid rock. The legs were a bas-relief of his ancestors holding aloft a giant beam for the grand chanter to sing the Songs of Sradda, the prayers of his people. Behind the religious leader was a wide block of wall, polished so that it mirrored the service taking place. It had cracked sometime when Aqin erupted, and as a result, the light refracted, allowing for one person to be multiplied into a hundred. V'sair looked up, seeing his face split in two, imitating his own internal schism.

He slid into his place, a pew just like the rest, nothing decorating it to make it special. Ornamentation could distract the pious from their sole purpose of communing with the Elements. A great pit with the eternal flame of the Elements burned bright, its orange and blue flames creating a show of dancer-like movements on the smooth surface. The shadows were compact and small, and as they traveled toward the rear of the temple, they stretched to become distorted images on the wall that seemed somehow threatening. The vast chamber echoed with the hiss and crackle of the flame. His father had stripped religious houses of all ostentatiousness, insisting that in the temple, all Darracians would be heard by the Elements equally.

He bowed, placing his head in his hands, praying for guidance. Positioning his fingers in the appropriate spot over his heart, he cleared his mind, letting his cares fall away so he could devote himself to finding solutions. V'sair concentrated on calling out to the Elements, picturing them, recalling the sound of Ozre's voice, feeling nothing, with the exception of his own desperation. He was missing something, his answer just out of his reach. It was as if it were one giant puzzle and the center was missing. The comet, Ozre, the non-stop rain—the solution was hovering before him in a jumble of answers that he could not sort out. He heard the echo of his whispers bounce off the polished clear walls, but no response was returned.

Chanter Brault gripped the chalice in his pudgy fingers. His lips thinned with rage, his eyes darting through the empty chapel. Weak sunlight filtered in from the tall, narrow windows, and he asked for a sign. It had been a close call, but nobody had talked. He was safe, and yet, the king was alone. Could he not finish the plan and kill him in the Temple of the Elements? Wind chimes called the faithful to prayer; the window of time would soon be lost. Brault reached under his robe to touch the hilt of his Fireblade, unused since he had been elevated to the temple. It was purely ceremonial now, and he wondered briefly, if he activated the flame, would it burn the red of his youth, or the new blue flame of Darracian justice?

He withdrew it, his eyes widening as it jumped to life, bathing his face vermillion, and he suddenly realized he didn't care about the color anymore. He had heard that the prisoners had died, taking with them the secret of his role in the overthrow, as well as the instigator of the assassination. He walked toward the chapel, his Fireblade humming at his side, just beneath his robe. Trembling with excitement, he thought it was almost too easy.

As if the king heard him, he looked up, his face innocent in its youth, and he smiled at the chanter. "Have you come to lead me to the Elements?" V'sair asked.

Brault's clammy hand gripped his weapon, his insides turning to jelly, feeling the fire of purpose die along with his courage. Blood would be on his hands;

they would know that it was he who did the deed, and perhaps the guards would overwhelm them. How would the new social order they had planned survive without his guidance? No, let someone else rid the Darracians of V'sair's liberal ideas. But then, if he rid the planet of this half-breed, he would be hailed a hero. Lothen might give him a title, some territory of his own…

Wiping a nervous hand across a sweat-dotted head, he looked at the altar and shuddered, thinking he had seen a movement. It couldn't be, he thought wildly, a trick of light, nothing more, but the image returned, and he found himself staring into the eyes of Drakko, V'sair's dead father. Gasping, he coughed, his eyes bulging from his gray face, now a pasty shade of green.

"Are you well?" V'sair stood to hold out a hand to help the older man.

Brault backed away with a slight bow, sliding his blade into his holster behind his back and then smiling with uncertainty. "Together we shall ask for guidance." Falling to his knees, he heard the door open and knew that V'sair's royal guards were taking seats in the rear. "Oh, Great Sradda, giver of life, I commend myself to thee…" He began the Songs of Sradda, his mind feverously working on a different solution.

Brault had lost his nerve, losing his chance to ignite the coup. He watched the king sideways, lost his prayer, his face illuminated by the great Fires of the Elements, and wondered what he had just witnessed. Never a warrior, he had chosen religion because he was afraid of fighting other Darracians. Only because of his well-placed family was he able to advance through the temple hierarchy. There were no such things as ghosts—it was his imagination, nothing more. He smiled to himself. He had made the right decision. If V'sair and Swart survived this, he would be their religious lodestone. If Lothen succeeded, then he would be seen as a great ally. Leave his holy hands clean. Let them find someone who had no need to wonder of ghosts or devils, to take the chance with their souls.

He knew there were other rebels out there, operating within unknown cells. To protect them from being discovered, only one person knew all the members of each group. That man was now dead, and Brault had no idea who else was involved. He just knew he had to sit tight. Help was on the way. Let Lothen or one of the others take the glory; he would be fine taking a backseat until it was safe.

"Oh Great Sradda"—his voice soared to the roof of the great temple—"show me the way to your light!" Who knew which way it was going to go? "Spare me to be useful to the victor, whomever he may be." Brault smiled at the king's bowed head.

IX

REMINDA'S BARE FEET slapped on the cold stone of the volcano. She was alone, her guards unhappily waiting outside. She secured her wrap around her small shoulders. Aqin was damp as well as cold. The rain dripped along the inside walls of a dead volcano whose fire had been extinguished.

The cavern was empty. Reminda seated herself with a sigh, hoping Tulani and Bobbien would return sometime soon. She eyed the small altar, then walked over and kneeled to place her tattooed forehead against the cold stone.

"Oh, great Ozre, I commend myself to thee. Return and speak." She paused, taking a deep breath. "I beg of thee…" she added in a whisper.

The cavern filled with wind, racing in a circular movement, lifting anything not attached to the floor.

Reminda held her dress down; it billowed beneath her palms. The wind was fierce, and the fabric ripped.

"You are angry with us?" she yelled, her blue eyes wide.

"Not angry, disappointed." The response filled the room, and a ball of light appeared in the center of the small tornado.

"So am I!" Reminda replied indignantly.

Ozre's laughter echoed off the walls. "Are you now?"

The gusts died, and the ball of light came close to Reminda's face. It hung inches from her, and she saw into the bright red core.

"You accuse your son of not having patience; we think the apple does not fall far from the tree."

"Perhaps," Reminda replied, exasperated. "That is not important! Why have you deserted us? V'sair is floundering, Tulani is lost, Zayden is wallowing, and I…"

"Yes?" the light said softly.

"You are the Element, Ozre. You know what I am."

"So you say…"

"Why?" Reminda implored.

"Why?" Ozre repeating, sounding exactly like her.

"Stop repeating everything I say!" Reminda demanded. "You upended our world, threw us head over heels by indicating all we believed in was not the truth."

"V'sair made that discovery, not us."

"But all of Darracia is reeling from this revelation. The roots for all their doctrine are based on their superiority, and the blinders have been removed for them to find that strength is drawn from our inner values."

"Isn't that what you wanted?" Ozre asked.

"Yes, yes, Drakko and I wanted V'sair to be supported as the king because he earned it through his strength of character."

"Then my job is finished," the Element said with finality.

"How can you say that?" Reminda held out her hand.

"He is struggling."

"No one said it was going to be easy," Ozre said reasonably.

"Well, yes, but…"

"It has not turned out precisely the way you expected," the ball purred as it caressed her head.

Reminda sighed, tears glistening in her eyes.

"There are other Elements, my dear, other Elements to fulfill your hopes. But they can help only when you reach out for them."

"I am reaching! How can I find Ereth?"

"Reach higher, deeper. I can't believe Ereth has been sending all of you signs; he is there for you. You are all so steeped in grief and unhappiness you cannot see what is right in front of your eyes."

Reminda's heart cracked within her chest as she fell to her knees; her pride evaporated like the morning dew. She felt the warmth of Ozre envelop her, and a knowing heat filled her body. Taking deep, absorbing breaths, she let the feeling of peace wash over her, her soul lifting up.

"I can feel you now, Ozre. Why?" she asked softly.

"This I can help you with, my dear. You are finally asking the right questions. I am the Element of earth."

The voice reverberated in her head, and she listened, tears running down her cheeks.

"I am the Element of truth, the direct path of mind

to heart. You know me, Reminda. You and the others have just lost your way."

"Sometimes when you are distracted by nonsense…"

A new voice spoke, and Reminda gasped, her hands over her mouth with joy. She rose slowly, turning to see her husband inside the shimmering ball of Ozre, young and handsome, his gaping wound gone.

"Drakko…" she whispered.

"I never left you, my love. I am right beside you." His voice filled her with serene joy, warming her to her cold feet.

"Drakko, beloved," she whispered.

"When your grief abates, you will see me and finish the work we set out to do."

She felt his voice like a warm balm to her soul.

"I miss you…" Words were inadequate, so she thought it instead, and her dead husband smiled.

The ball of light expanded, and she felt its comfort invade her body. She covered herself with both arms, trying to hold on to the feeling, as his voice vibrated inside of her.

"I am always with you, my life. I would never leave you or my sons. You have let emotions cloud reason, and because of this, you are all failing in your missions."

Reminda gasped as his hands covered her heart; closing her eyes, she relaxed into his embrace. For a second, she could smell him; she inhaled, trying to attach him to her.

Drakko chuckled. "You don't have to do that. Strip your fears. Wash away doubt, and open your mind to see things as they really should be. Tell our son I understand how he feels and he is on the right path. I support his decisions. When I was in the physical, I thought I knew everything, but now I really do, and he is on the right track. Tell him not to ignore his heart, that the Elements are with him. If he opens his eyes, he will see the answers right before him. Know that I love you, Reminda, and you have always been the best part of me…" His voice started to fade.

"Noooo…don't leave," she wailed.

"I must. You have work to do yet, and then you will understand. Search your heart, and you will feel me."

The ball winked and disappeared, leaving Reminda in total darkness.

The queen sank to the floor, her face wet with tears. Curled into a tight ball, she felt her heart expand. He was not gone, just in a place where she could not see him. If she did what she had to do, then they would be united. She felt lighter than she had in a year; the grief had lifted. She saw a mountain to climb in her head; now she knew what she had to do. Caught up in her own thoughts, she didn't hear Tulani enter the cave, her braids hanging limply from the rain.

Tulani fell to her knees. "Highness." She bowed her head reverently.

Reminda looked up, her face serene, holding out her arms. "Tulani, I have missed you."

The girl needed no more invitation. She rushed into the queen's embrace as if Reminda were her long-lost mother.

<u>**X**</u>

NAJE CRUSHED THE magon beetles to make a paste for Lord Nuen's wound. He was bound to be irritable tonight; she knew he hated drinking with Lothen. They were leaving tonight on Lothen's lead ship, traveling to Darracia. In the privacy of their rooms, he complained about the climate, the food, the customs. She knew he missed his home, perhaps even what was left of his family. They didn't share much. Glancing at the floor, she spied a box of graphen packets sticking out. Cursing softly, she kicked at it gently, pushing it in so it wouldn't be seen. She planned on taking them on board the ship, and that was definitely against the law. Pausing, she reached down, took a few of them, and slid them underneath her shirt, next to her breast. Dangerous, yes, but necessary, and at least she was armed somewhat. If she threw them against a wall with force, they would explode, giving her some sort of security.

She parted the curtains to look at the dying light, wondering if her sister knew she was relatively safe. Poor Denita, how would she manage without her? Denita was the youngest, though she was not a child, but she knew nothing of graphen or the business of a den. The graphen den did not belong to her. Denita was always the protected one. They had wanted a better life for her; Naje had been saving to get her off the planet and into an academy. Anything but staying on the cesspit they called home. After their parents died in the Fever of '27, she sold their butcher stalls. They had been one of the numerous purveyors of different meats on Venturian. Denita moved into the back of her sister's den. It wasn't what anybody wanted. It was a dirty trade, and she wasn't proud of it.

The business had been purchased by her husband, Racin, killed, like her dreams, by his dependence on the drug, leaving her a poor widow running a vice-infested store. Did she miss him, she wondered, cocking her head, her dark hair falling to the side of her face. She supposed not. They had married young, before they really knew each other. She had wanted to get away from the meat stalls, her overbearing father, and escape to start her life. Well, the graphen den was no escape, especially when Racin started using. He became addicted so quickly, so thoroughly, that soon he was smoking more than they could afford. Oh, she could have left him, but for what, to go home and tell her father he was right? Instead, she ran the shop, widowed young and cutting the graphen to make it stretch. She almost welcomed the invaders when they took her away.

Slicing some fruit, she knew it would refresh Nuen and perhaps put him in a better mood. He thought he was tough, Lord Nuen. Cried like a baby when she didn't give him graphen. She had this forbidden stash of it hidden away. Highly unstable, it was not allowed on anything except for transport vehicles; certainly they'd kill her if they knew she had some on a royal barge. She could blow them all to Venturian and back with the amount she had.

Staf was easy to handle now that she knew his inner demons. Compared to the animals she handled in the graphen den, he was putty in her hands. As long as she anticipated his needs, he was relatively easy. She played up her hatred in front of Lothen, though. She would die before submitting to him again. The Planta leader was vicious, cunning and without a soul. She hated him and would have killed him if she could have found a way. He was as ruthless as he was deceitful, and she knew nobody should turn their back on him.

The door slid open, and Staf entered without a word. He grunted some sort of greeting as he threw himself into his chair. Naje reached forward wordlessly to remove his boots and smiled slyly at his sigh of relief. Staf rolled his head back on the cushion, his eyes bleary.

"Your head aches, my lord?"

She placed her cool hands on his temples and kneaded them. His eyes were too yellow, and if he didn't stop, he would soon be too far gone with graphen. Though he was relaxed, his sharp eyes observed her.

"I don't know why I like you."

"Don't you?" she asked, and smiled at Staf.

"I was married to a princess. Beatha was granddaughter to a king."

"You can call a hag a beautiful." Naje shrugged. "But at the end of the day, she is still a hag."

Staf laughed, grabbed her hand, and kissed her wrist.

"Indeed, she was a hag." He pulled her onto his lap.

"I am not a princess." Naje eyed him, pulling away.

Staf hugged her against him. "But you are beautiful." He kissed her full on the mouth, smiling with triumph as her lips softened. "So beautiful."

"But, alas"—she raised herself, holding his head with both her hands—"still a slave."

"You are mine," Staf whispered possessively, and the discussion was finished.

◆

Mere hours later Staf found himself on the bridge of Lothen's light cruiser. The Plantan leader had three ships under his command as he embarked on the two-day journey to Darracia. Naje watched Planta shrink as they ate up the miles to deeper space. She was happy to see the back end of it. It was a filthy place, the sea a churning mass of acid, the landmass a tiny wasteland. It rivaled Venturian for its lack of charm, and although a better climate, the recent global warming from the pollution had made going outside impossible.

The ships flew in a defensive formation, the king in the lead vessel. They were by no means large or considered capable of intergalactic travel, but they were able to land stealthily on the sea, surprising and then destroying their victims before they had a chance to retaliate. The ships were triangular, with easy maneuverability. They were known to zip in, create panic, steal what they needed, and take what they wanted. The Plantans painted the bows of their ships with fantastical creatures with frightening expressions. With mostly a male crew, Lothen balked when Staf insisted on taking Naje.

"She is a slave, my lord. You will get another," Lothen told him.

"I don't want another," Staf replied with finality.

He kept her in his quarters, away from the bloodthirsty crew. Naje happily complied. She was there when Staf swaggered in, high from graphen, furious with Lothen for encouraging its use. Already, she had seen the Darracian's hands shaking when he needed the drug, and although she warned him with long looks, he ignored her pleas. She shouldn't care, she knew, but oddly enough, she liked him. He had an aura of power; as opposed to the waste of a male she had had for a husband, she felt that with Staf she had a future, if he didn't kill himself with graphen first. As long as she kept him under control, he'd be fine. She shrugged. If he needed the drug, she would get it for him, but on her terms and in the dose that would keep him under her thumb and useful.

"What is the matter, my lord?" she asked as he stared sullenly out the portal into deep space.

"Geva. What do you know of their Geva?"

"I know nothing." She kneeled and took hold of his face as he reclined on his chair. "And neither do you!" she said urgently.

"She is foul and evil. Please," Naje begged him, "do not go to her altar."

Staf sighed as he looked bleakly out the window.

"Staf," she whispered, "she will steal your soul…"

XI

"I CAN ARRANGE for a transport to take you to the surface, Your Majesty." The stable master followed V'sair as he leaped into Hother's saddle.

"No. I told you, I am going riding." V'sair dismissed him, turning his mount toward the openings. It was still pouring. He didn't care. His mother had gone down to the surface hours ago; he was going after her. He was sick of Syos and all of its inhabitants. He had just come from another meeting with Chanter Brault, and their heated argument frustrated V'sair. It had started innocently enough, first with a service in the temple, followed by a discussion in the chanter's office. He respected the counselor about as much as the chanter liked V'sair. He missed the steady influence of Emmicus. Something in the older man's eyes made him uneasy, and V'sair was beginning to have a decided lack of trust in him.

It was the same old thing as far as the young king was concerned. The chanter was white with rage over the idea of a Quyroo crowning him. V'sair was tired of it all. Nothing was smooth. Even the relationship with his father's most loyal servant, General Swart, felt strained. He knew the old man meant well; it was just that his ideas were antiquated. He was clinging to the obsolete notion of the Fireblade and Darracian strength. Sometimes it was too hard to keep swimming against the tide. He missed Tulani and her comforting arms with an intenseness that bordered on pain.

He turned to the four guards saddling their stalliuses behind him. "No! You are to stay here," he ordered them.

"Sorry, Highness." One of them bowed his head respectfully. "We've been ordered to stay close to you by General Swart."

"It's fine. I will be fine, and I dismiss you."

"He will have our heads." The soldier shrugged, his eyes forlorn. "We will keep a distance," he offered, his palm up.

V'sair gave in as ungraciously as any twenty-year-old feeling burdened by unwanted watchdogs. "If you must." He wheeled out of the stables quickly, smiling at his deft maneuvering, thinking he had lost them for a minute. The sky was deserted, the weather making most travel impossible. He heard the labored breathing of their mounts when they tried to make up the growing distance, Hother easily outdistancing them as she ate up the miles.

The rain stopped and the sky brightened, the dual

rays of Rast and Nost creating a halo of light. A rainbow sprang up over Syos, painting the horizon a multicolored hue that framed the dormant volcano. He guided Hother toward the Desa. Brilliant sunlight blinded him momentarily; he heard the whickers of several stalliuses behind him. They said they would keep their distance, he thought with fury. He spun, rigid with anger, to come face-to-face with General Vekin, his father's other trusted advisor. The older man had never recovered from the battle for Darracia. His left arm hung uselessly at his side. He had lost three of his sons, leaving him without an heir. A fog of sadness surrounded him. His voice, raspy from a wound to his throat, stopped V'sair's progress to escape.

"Relax, Highness." The older man halted him with a raised hand. "Cannot you spare some conversation for an old friend?" He paused and gazed at the young man. "We used to be good friends, V'sair."

V'sair tapped his pommel and sidled up next to the wizened man. He smiled warmly to the wrinkled face, fond memories of playing soldier with the general reminding him of the relationship.

General Vekin motioned for his own men to leave. "Give us space." He motioned for them to fly in a formation a bit away from them.

Together they began a leisurely flight, their stalliuses gliding together in a ballet of synchronization. They floated through the pink and orange clouds, above the condensation, so that they heard the muffled sounds of the Desa beneath them. Hanging in suspension, they galloped over the Hixom Sea, watching the flying fish jump into the wet atmosphere.

"This weather seems to be here for good," the general observed.

"It makes the Desa bloom." V'sair pointed to the lush red foliage populating the hills. It appeared even denser than his last visit. Tulani was down there somewhere.

"You always find the good in everything, V'sair," Vekin stated kindly, then sighed.

"What troubles you, General?"

"I have news." The general reached into his tunic and pulled out a white paper.

V'sair reached across to take the paper. He read it quickly, then crumbled it into a tight ball, his mouth down turned into a narrow white line. "I am not surprised," he said through gritted teeth.

"I don't know how much time you have, but you must act quickly." General Vekin grabbed his arm.

"You are with me?" V'sair looked him full in the face.

"You had to ask?" The general's stallius moved restlessly as she neighed.

"I have to get my mother. I will be back very soon."

Vekin wheeled his mount toward the castle gleaming in the suns, the polished surface blinding his eyes. "I will mobilize."

V'sair held out his hand, clasping the general's in a firm embrace. "I will never forget this."

Vekin nodded and turned to the castle.

XII

V'SAIR URGED HOTHER downward toward the hills leading to the hulking great outline of Aqin. It was raining in earnest, and he was soaked, the chill creeping under his tunic to settle in his bones.

He landed hard in the mud, Hother skidding, coming to rest up to her knees in the soft earth of the planet. She looked like a different animal, her white coat speckled red, like a wild hybrid stallius. After jumping off, he sank deeply to his thighs. Rain dripped off the canopy of leaves to run in icy tracks under the back of his shirt. His white hair was plastered to his forehead; his clothes stuck to him like a second skin. He looked around to get his bearings, unsure because of the dense gloom. The Desa was hushed, the rain pattered on the leaves, and V'sair heard nothing, not a bird, frog, or keewalla monkey. Wrapping the reins around his hand, he whispered for

Hother to follow him up the steep incline toward the secret entrance Bobbien had taught him to use.

If it was quiet before, it became deathly still, not a breeze, as if the entire world was holding its breath. Even the gentle whine of insects ceased. V'sair turned his head, trying to figure out what he was hearing. A roar as loud as a thousand cannon rent the air, getting closer. V'sair spun, his feet stuck in the mud, only to lose his balance and fall hard on his elbows. In the distance he saw a rushing wall of water, as if the bowels of the earth had opened. It was a swirling mass, its sound magnified by the echoing wall of the canyon until it deafened him. V'sair opened his mouth in a soundless scream; he pulled at his feet, which uselessly sank, trapped in muddy shackles.

He looked around wildly, knowing there was no escape. Turning, he slapped Hother hard on the butt. She reared, her eyes rolling, but wouldn't leave. "I will weigh you down, you stupid beast!" He grabbed a stick and whipped her flank, watching with relief as she opened her vast wings to lift off above the impending disaster. He pointed upward, and his mount obeyed. V'sair watched sadly as his only avenue of escape floated upward.

The water shook the ground, and the spray splashed his face. Licking his lips, he realized it was salty, and he wondered where the seawater was coming from. Turning to meet his destiny, ready to accept fate head-on, he stared boldly at the churning mass of gray seawater barreling through the Desa, flattening everything in its path save the oldest and strongest of the trees. Taking a deep breath, he parted his mouth to meet the Great Sradda with a song on his lips, when he was grabbed under the armpits and lifted violently, his feet sucked out of the thick mud painfully. Airborne, he tried to turn his head but saw only that it was a Quyroo male and he was being propelled through the tangle of vines at a dizzying speed.

"Who are you?" he called out, watching the force of water travel on a destructive path toward the volcano. He heard only labored breathing and knew he had been snatched from impending death by this savior.

The Quyroo slowed, coming to rest in the lee of a tree that was so tall it grazed the clouds. V'sair looked up, seeing Hother circling above them, a smile splitting his face. He started to laugh and heard the Quyroo laugh right along with him, their bodies shaking with relief. He felt the weight of the branch dip and knew another Quyroo had joined them.

"This is getting to be too much, my lord," a familiar voice told him.

"Bobbien!" he shouted with joy. He turned to identify the man holding him. "Do I know you?" "Your Majesty." The officer bowed.

"I do not think we have met." V'sair studied his handsome face. He was big, his royal infantry uniform stretched across impossibly large shoulders.

"I am Seren." The huge Quyroo nodded.

"I have to get to the volcano—my mother is there." V'sair reached out for a vine to leave.

The native shook his head. "I am sorry, my lord. There is no way to get there until the water recedes.

This area is my responsibility. General Vekin asked me to watch out for you. I saw you and the stallius on the mountain ridge struggling with the mud."

"No." V'sair tried to free himself of the iron grip. The talon-like hands held fast. "My mother…"

"I am sorry, Your Majesty. We have to wait for the water to leave before we can examine the volcano entrance. It is unsafe. Those are my orders."

"You think I don't want to go there?" Bobbien demanded, grabbing the front of his tunic, her face pink with fear. "Tulani is down there too," she choked out, her voice thick. "Watch, watch. The water is leaving." She pointed with her staff.

XIII

DENITA FUMED ANGRILY as Zayden's capable hands belted her properly into her seat. "Let me out of here, you oversized ape. I should have let you die back there!" she spit angrily.

Zayden cinched the belt tighter, laughing when Denita turned as red as a Quyroo. He chucked her under the chin, which only inflamed her. "I'm taking you to my stepmother."

"Over my dead body."

"That could be arranged," Zayden replied as he jumped into his seat. The engines roared to life, and once again he heard Denita pounding the glass partition. "What…What…? I can't hear you." He chuckled, placing his headset over his ears. He did hear her curses and took off steeply, knowing she was pressed uncomfortably in her seat. That ought to shut her up, he thought, hearing the screams change to retching. *Not a great flyer, our Denita.* He smiled as he steered his compact ship toward the rising suns of Darracia.

They drifted through the nebula, Zayden enjoying the peace of the void of space. It was a small ship and made a lot of people nervous—not much metal separated a passenger from the nothingness of the outside. Zayden felt lighter for the first time in a while. Much to his relief, Denita's screams had died down to sullen silence. He admitted he felt a bit bad for her. He was an independent person and understood her need to control her own life, but he was going to go after Staf, and he couldn't do it with an encumbrance. He knew he could really dump her anywhere. She was a big girl; it was also clear she could fend for herself. If only he didn't feel so responsible for her.

"Look, General. I'll spring your sister. What's her name?" The silence had finally gotten to him, and he threw out a peace offering.

"I don't need your help, Warrior. When I get the chance, I'm going to finish what the Plantans started!" she shouted, her face a mask of rage.

He looked at her indulgently and replied, "You're kind of cute when you're mad."

She sputtered furiously, "I don't need your stinking Fireblade—I'm going to kill you with these!" She held up her clenched hands, her face a grimace.

"Get in line, General," he replied as he swung left, heading toward the haven of home.

♦

They observed a few convoys, mostly truckers hauling products from one end of the solar system to the other. Many of the planets had to rely on these outsourced vendors. Most of the societies weren't rich enough for more than just the wealthy to have ships. On Darracia, only the richest had ships that could travel outside the atmosphere of their own home, let alone travel to other planets. Zayden lazed the day away, making notes on weather conditions, and pulled into Pagil 7 to refuel. It was a rowdy space station owned by a bigshot company outside their solar system. He remembered that his father had negotiated rates with them, and though he felt a lump in his throat, it didn't pack the punch it had when he thought about him before. In fact, he realized with surprise, he hadn't thought about Hilde for a few days either. He looked back at Denita's angry face, asked if she wanted to grab a bite, and told her it wouldn't have to be silver crab.

They disembarked; Zayden lifted Denita from her seat, marveling at her tiny waist. A mechanic rushed past him, pushing the big Darracian. Zayden grabbed Denita close to him to prevent them both from falling. The world narrowed to the two of them as her hands gripped his shoulders tightly. Denita's tongue touched her lips, her eyes holding Zayden's in a lock more powerful than a force field. Her long-lashed eyes closed for an instant, and he leaned forward to caress her lips with his own, lightly grazing her. Denita grabbed his braid to pull his face close to kiss him with a desperation born from lone-liness. Zayden's hard body wrapped naturally around her softer one. Their skin melted together as though it had familiar memories matching up like puzzle pieces cut exclusively for the other.

The sound of the bustling terminal coupled with the cry of "Get a room already!" broke the mood, and Zayden felt his face heat with embarrassment. He low-ered her to the floor, took her hand, and said, "I'm sorry. I didn't mean to do that."

Denita looked him hard in the face and replied, "Well, I did."

The restaurant was typical spaceport food—greasy mys-tery products from all ends of the galaxy and just about as old. Zayden approached her with a tray laden with an array of products, but they picked over the disgusting containers and smelly wrapping, hardly eating at all.

"The food here is prehistoric." Zayden hit the table with stale bread, watching bugs march fearlessly across the surface to feast on his crumbs.

Denita's face curled into a disgusted frown, and he marveled at her tiny nose, thinking it made her adorable. She wasn't a bad-looking female, he mused. In fact—he watched her intently—she was rather beautiful.

He sipped his steaming chay, while Denita drank the beverage native to her home, a white, overly sweet liquid that made his bile rise.

Denita watched his stern face softening and figured she might have a shot at making him take her. "You have to take me with you," she informed him over the din of the place. "It's not safe. I can't worry about you and do what needs to be done. Look," he said with a conciliatory smile, "you're going to like Reminda. She's a great lady, and besides, how many of your friends can say they hung out with a queen?"

"I don't have any friends. You need me." She pounded the table, her brown eyes imploring him. She had a white mustache rimming her lips, and Zayden's own eye caressed her face. Reaching out, he wiped her top lip with a gentle finger.

"I wish I could, but it's just not safe. I will bring your sister back to you. I promise."

He purchased her a change of clothing and arranged for them both to be able to bathe. Her boots were shot from the sand of Fon Reni, so he replaced them too. He left her at the female spa while he went to the baths for a cleanup as well. He didn't want to deliver a ragamuffin to his stepmother, and he wondered why it suddenly mattered so much. Zayden's fingers touched the tattoo embedded in his shoulder. The swirls beckoned him with the same hypnotic effect as the desire in Denita's eyes. Closing his eye, he pictured her creamy caramel skin, accepting the responsibility to keep her safe. He would never let a female put herself in harm's way again. He allowed himself to be shaved and his hair trimmed, and enjoyed the steaming water more than he had expected.

Denita gave herself up to the fancy, high-priced attendants. She had never been so pampered in all her life.

Venturian was so cold that rarely did one get a

chance to bathe more than one part of the body. Hair was washed monthly, the cost of heating water too dear.

The perfumed water coated her skin, making it feel and look like a golden pelt. Her hair floated silkily, and when they came to take her out, she refused the first time, enjoying the cocooning warmth of the steaming bath. She sat in the pool, listening to the piped-in music, wondering how she was ever going to return to Venturian. Cupping her hands, she poured a waterfall of soapy liquid over her head, inhaling the flowery essence, thinking of Zayden's soft lips and the way his hands had felt as he held her against him. Her skin tingled with desire, yet she was angry at Zayden. There was no way she was going to let him go to Planta without her. She realized with a start that she couldn't live if something happened to him.

They met outside the spa, and Zayden blinked, his amber eye wide with surprise. Denita's hair framed her café au lait face, feathered in a new style. He had thought her hair black but now realized there was a symphony of browns and golds streaking through the wavy locks. She wore a tight gray pantsuit that emphasized her coltish legs.

"Denita, you look…good." Zayden swallowed.

Denita stared at his wide shoulders encased in a darkblue tunic. He was so tall, his powerful tail peeking through the back of his pants. Denita reached up to touch his scarred face. Zayden pulled away, but she placed her palm gently on the ruined skin, her fingers leaving a trail of gentleness in their wake. Zayden closed his eye, and when he opened it, it was to see Denita's face close to his own. Her lips pressed against his, and he felt her lips moving.

"You are mine, Warrior, and don't you forget it."

He grabbed her hand, walking briskly to his ship. He had to get her to Reminda, and fast.

XIV

STAF'S YELLOWED EYES observed the large screen in Lothen's bridge. The Plantan leader sat in his chair, his long legs stretched out before him. They didn't allow graphen on the ship, yet Naje had managed to smuggle some on board, and he smoked it alone in his quarters. He smiled thinking of her seductive smile and sultry eyes.

"We will be passing the space station momentarily." Lothen pointed to a huge doughnut-shaped wheel rotating in a circle.

"It's a dump." Staf laughed. "Don't drink the chay. I hear it's made from recycled piss."

"Everything is recycled. I wouldn't eat anything there," Lothen agreed.

This, coming from a being who ate live species

from his planet, made Staf laugh with abandon. Lothen watched him coolly.

"We amuse you, my lord?"

"More than you realize," Staf acknowledged.

"Perhaps you will share what humors you?" Lothen asked in the deathly silence of the bridge.

The station was surrounded by docked ships. Staf had been watching as some attached themselves for a landing and others departed in many different ways. It was an important way station, and he and his brother had argued over it for years. He had wanted a piece of the profits. It bordered Darracian territory. Drakko wouldn't hear of it. He didn't want the responsibility; his brother only worried about the Quyroos and their issues. He never saw the bigger picture. A small craft detached from the landing bay, its tight lines and green and blue stripes unmistakable. Staf leaned forward, his hands gripping a rail, a growl erupting from his throat.

"Look." Staf pointed to a small ship leaving the spaceport. "It cannot be…"

Lothen sat forward to observe. "What is it, my lord?"

"Zayden! I would know his ship anywhere."

"Who?"

"The king's bastard, Zayden of Darracia. Get him!" he ordered, superseding Lothen's authority.

The helmsman glanced in question to the king, who nodded in assent. "Follow them. Now!"

◆

Zayden looked up and did a double take when he realized a painted Plantan cruiser was bearing down on him at a dangerous speed. Flipping his switches to fire up his turbos, he called back to Denita, "Hang on! This may get bumpy." Pressing the throttle to the max, he felt his spine press back into the curve of his seat as the ship jumped into its hyperspeed. The stars elongated into white strips as he zipped into a vortex of speed, hoping to escape the murderous intent of the enemy ship.

Glancing backward, he realized the Plantans had not only followed him but were fast eating up the distance to his ship. With more powerful engines, they overpowered him, and his craft lurched as a powerful tractor beam attached itself, then started to pull them into its gaping maw.

Zayden wondered why the Plantans had targeted him. While they were lifelong enemies, they seldom bothered with small recreational craft, waiting to attack the fatter pickings of the large cargo ships. Well, he thought with chagrin, V'sair would just have to pay the ransom. Then he would be free once more to resume his search for Staf.

The ship was sucked into a landing bay, and once he saw Plantans surround his ship, he knew the atmosphere had been normalized. He pressed the mechanism to open the glass hood, unstrapped himself, and climbed onto the wing of his ship.

"What do you want from me?" Zayden demanded.

"That depends," came the gravelly baritone he knew so well. "That depends on how much you are willing to take."

A shot rang out, and Zayden heard a scream, but as he tumbled from his ship, he didn't remember if it was Hilde's or Denita's.

XV

"I HAVE MISSED you so, child." Reminda held Tulani's face in her hands and kissed both her cheeks.

"Oh, Your Majesty, me too!" Tulani replied, her eyes glistening with tears. "I think I am ready to join you. Maybe I can accomplish more from Syos than I can from here." She paused, her face horror-struck as if a thought had just occurred to her. "I mean, that is, if you still want me?"

"Want you?" Reminda smiled. "Silly girl. If V'sair doesn't marry you, I will!" Reminda laughed at the absurdity.

"I cannot break the barriers here; they will not accept me as one of their own."

"I understand more than you realize, Tulani," Reminda said sympathetically. The rain battered against the walls of the volcano, and she shivered. Turning her head toward a sound, she asked, "What is that?"

Tulani stood, looking at the mouth of the tunnel. "I don't know. It sounds like a mudslide." She pressed her ear to the wall, but did not feel the heat of Ozre, or recognize the new sound.

"Oh heavenly Sradda!" Reminda's eyes widened in her pale face. "Look!"

A wall of water was rushing through the corridors of the volcano, bright green with ocean foam. Uprooted red trees floated in eddies of the whirlpools. There was no other escape; they were trapped, Tulani thought wildly. The safety of Aqin had turned into a prison. Tulani raced to a forest of stalagmites to climb to safety. She reached out to Reminda.

"Hurry! Get as high as you can go!" she called out over the deafening sound of rushing water.

Reminda's personal guard swirled in, reaching out to cling to anything that would hold them. She heard their helpless shouts and watched them tumble out of view. Tulani grabbed Reminda's wrist, and using her Quyroo strength, she hauled her up, almost losing her as the water gushed through the cavern in a violent wave.

"Hold on," she cried out as she climbed up the stalagmite, her fingernails tearing as she scraped them against the hard surface. Reminda's face was white as fallen snow, her hand just as cold. She shook her, urging, "Stay with me, Your Highness...Reminda!"

She pulled her up so they were face-to-face, clinging to the structure. The queen's eyes had narrowed to slits, a cut high on her cheek, blood flowing freely. As their feet dangled, the water surged higher, until they were covered to their chins. Water invaded their mouths; they both retched and choked, pushing up their chins to escape the rising tide. Reminda slipped under the foamy seawater. Tulani scrambled to get her back, but the queen disappeared under the swirling mass of violent waves.

"Oh no," she wailed, holding tight to her stalagmite, her skin rubbed raw by the abrasive surface. Sobs racked her body, and she pressed her face into the damp rock, angry. She cursed the Elements, she cursed Ozre, and she cried for her lost friend. The air was sucked out of the room as she inched higher to the ceiling, the water dangerously close to her mouth. Light-headed and weak with grief, she held on to the structure, her body wrapped so tightly she shivered with numbing cold. A webbed hand grabbed her arm, and Tulani screamed as if a thousand wysbies had stung her. The manicured fingers squeezed her encouragingly, and she turned around, reaching down to press her shoulder into the queen's armpit.

"Oh, my lady, are you all right?"

"Did you forget," Reminda choked out between spasms of coughing, "did you forget I yet have my gills?"

"Gills?" Tulani asked stupidly, her long lashes crusted with the salt from the ocean water.

"I am Plantan. We have gills. However, life in the clouds has weakened them. What's happening?" Reminda gasped.

"I don't know. Great, sweet Sradda, preserve us. Ozre, Ozre save us!" Tulani's voice echoed off the wet wall of the cavern.

"Courage, child" reverberated inside her head. The

water tickled the lower lip of her mouth; she gagged on the saltiness of it. Their heads were pressed to the ceiling of the chamber, the sound of their ragged breaths echoing above the waterline. The entire room was phosphorus from the minerals in the water.

"Oh Ozre, why have you forsaken me?" she asked.

The water began to recede with a great sucking sound. It pulled, dragging both Reminda and Tulani. Their arms ached from holding on, yet they stayed glued to the safety of their perches. Debris banged into them, injuring and ripping skin. Reminda heard her ribs crack, yet Tulani's soft prayers kept her holding on, despite the pain.

Soon, only the damp sound of dripping water filled the small space. They heard the tide being pulled out of the cave, and Ozre's bright light lit up their space. Tulani and the queen dropped, exhausted, to the soaking floor, their breathing harsh in the cold air.

"Do you hear me now?" Ozre demanded and disappeared, leaving them in pitch darkness.

◆

They heard V'sair's cries before they saw him. He was running into the cave, Bobbien right behind him, and a passel of Quyroo guards following. He paused at the mouth of the room, his clothes sopping wet, to double over, his hands on his knees, while he caught his breath, relief evident on his young face. Standing, he held out his arms, and both women wordlessly ran to his embrace. "You are unharmed?" he asked quietly after kissing each of their heads.

Tulani nodded but kept her face buried in his shoulder. Tears filled her eyes at his familiar smell, the warmth of his arms, the concern in his voice. *I am home,* she thought, and didn't realize she had spoken aloud until V'sair answered her, his voice a rumble in his chest. "Finally."

Bobbien went to aid a groaning soldier, motioning for the other Quyroos to help.

V'sair looked at his mother. "Are you all right?"

"I will need Bobbien to tape my ribs—no, stop, Vsos. It is nothing I can't handle. Let her see to my men first."

"Have you any idea what this was about?" V'sair asked.

Reminda looked around. "Yes…no, I am not sure. I have to think about it a bit. But let's go home—we have much to discuss."

Tulani looked at V'sair with wonder. He kissed her gently on her lips.

"I have missed you." His voice bounced off the walls of the cavern.

Tulani opened her mouth to answer him, but another gaze caught her attention. Seren stared at her, his star-shaped eyes menacing with hatred. Tulani shuddered, burying her face in V'sair's shoulder.

"You are safe, my love."

Tulani whispered that she hoped so.

XVI

A DEVIL WAS jumping from one end of Zayden's skull to the other. He heard a moan, wincing at its depths of agony, then caught his breath when he realized it came from him.

A familiar, cool hand pressed on his clammy forehead, and he heard Denita whisper, "Don't show you are awake, yet. I hear them coming."

Zayden explored their surroundings through a slit lid. He didn't need his eye to know that they were in the bowels of a ship, the great hum of randam crystals loud in their ears. Still, he glanced around, puzzled.

"It's Plantans," Denita informed him, reading his thoughts. "Shhhhh…"

He heard the door slide open, followed by the sound of booted feet.

Denita felt him tense; she reached around to press down on his shoulders, reminding him to stay quiet.

"Is he up yet?" The hated voice filled the room.

Zayden swallowed the bile that rose to the back of his throat. His body vibrated with anger, but he held himself still.

"Not yet, my lord." Zayden heard Denita's humble voice. Humble? What had they done to her—she was afraid of nothing. She squeezed him reassuringly, and he wondered what her game was.

A hand pressed down on his chest, testing his response, but he looked inward, willing himself not to move a muscle. They moved upward to clutch his face, roughly turning it as if to observe his injury. He bit back a groan, keeping silent.

"I don't like it, Staf. He's been out too long." It was a new voice, but Zayden dared not glimpse at the speaker.

"It is a serious wound, sire," Denita offered, bowing her head. "I am not a healer. His eyes move but do not open. Perhaps your bullet struck true, and he will sleep forever?"

"It is a graze only." Staf dismissed her explanation. "I know of a healer on board. She understands the ways of these things."

Zayden heard them leave, and waited a few minutes until Denita's voice cut through the pain.

"They are gone, Warrior. You can get up now."

"Some warrior I turned out to be. I couldn't even keep you safe," Zayden replied as he eased into a seated position. Black dots swam before his eyes, and he wondered if he was about to pass out again.

Denita's heart did a little flip-flop when she realized he meant to protect her, not bully her. Oh why, why, why did she not trust others' intentions? she thought ruefully.

"Oh, your nose is bleeding again!" He felt tender hands cup the bottom of his head and lean him backward to slow the bleeding. "You are a proper mess, Zayden." She chuckled. "No, don't get up yet, you dummy."

"Yes, sir, General, sir!" He gave her a half-fast salute, which pained his forehead. "Ow…ow…ow…" His eyes were closed, and he was startled when he felt her soft lips caress his.

"Better?"

Despite the pain, Zayden reached out to pull her closer to kiss her fully on the lips, their arms entwined. Denita rested her forehead against his, then kissed him again.

"Oh, this is nice!" A voice interrupted them, pulling them apart, Denita's face lighting up with joy. "Just what are your intentions with my sister?" the stunning woman demanded from the doorway.

"Naje!" Denita ran to her sister, grabbing her around the waist, tears of happiness springing to her brown eyes.

Naje hugged her fiercely, her gimlet eyes watching Zayden, who observed with a reddening face. Closing the door, she held her sister at arm's length, asking, "What are you doing here, and with a Darracian?" She glanced at the long, messy braid dangling down his back. "And a royal one at that?"

"Royal? Zayden?"

"Hardly royal." Zayden stood painfully, gripping the cot as the room spun.

"Sit…Zayden, is it?" she examined the bloody crease above his ear. "Are you Drakko's get? Oh, don't tighten up on me, you numskull. Even out in Venturian we've heard about you."

"Drakko?"

"This is the king of the Darracians' firstborn, not the prince, Denita. This is his natural son. Hold still. This is going to sting a bit."

She poured something sharp smelling over the wound near his ear, and Zayden arched with a hiss; his eyes rolled backward, and he fell forward. The women caught him with easy hands and slid him back onto the cot. Naje checked his pulse, gave a satisfied nod, and sat down on the side of the bed.

"He's out," Naje said to her little sister. "Now tell me what's going on."

Denita explained her past few weeks and then asked her sister to relay what had happened to her.

"You don't seem like a prisoner to me," Denita accused Naje, who then covered her hand affectionately.

"I would have gotten word to you if I could, Denita. Make no mistake." She got up to wrap a bandage around Zayden's head. "I am a slave here. I have no rights, but Staf has been good to me."

"You are still a slave!"

"Was I not a slave to my husband, Racin? Do you think I loved him or that horrible graphen den? Do you think I liked peddling death?"

"You are still a slave…" Denita repeated. "But no matter. I am here, and we escape together."

"You will have to. Staf means to kill you both." Naje stood. "I cannot let that happen. Do you love him?"

Denita shrugged. "What is love?"

"If you have to ask, then I have my answer," Naje told her sister. "I will let Staf kill this one and let you go," she told her matter-of-factly.

Denita grabbed her arm. "No! I…You can't. He…I won't let him die."

"So the cold Venturian heart can speak. Yes, Sister. I will have to think of something to save both you and your fallen hero."

She exited quickly, leaving Denita to wonder what else her cold Venturian heart would have to say.

◆

"I have waited so long for this. Why does not the bastard wake?" Staf demanded as he sucked the smoke from the ever-present graphen pipe.

Naje shrugged. "Why have you this need for revenge?" She came close, wrapping her arms around his midsection.

He was mean and arbitrary, and Naje did not understand why she was drawn to him. She worried her bottom lip. "Can't you forget? There are places, my lord… There are places we can go to forget."

"What are you talking about?"

Naje pressed herself against him, holding both him and her secret close, and whispered against the back of his strong shoulder, "I am a slave to the Plantans." She rested her chin against him, trying to see his reaction, but his face was elusive. She watched the muscles tighten under his beard.

She heard a soft reply: "You are not a slave to me."

Emboldened, she went on, "As long as I am near a Plantan, I will be seen as a slave."

"You are my woman. You will be my consort."

"But not your queen." She moved away to turn and look him full in the face. "I have no future. I see no future for me. You will contract a royal marriage. Lothen will see you married to one of his pig-faced daughters. I will die alone."

Staf grabbed her by both arms. "Stop this talk! Stop it instantly!"

"I may be Lothen's slave," Naje hissed, "but I will not be yours!" She yanked free and ran from the room, leaving Staf with his graphen and his thoughts.

XVII

"I DON'T QUITE understand what Ozre was telling me," Reminda told her son from the confines of her room. "I have searched my mind but cannot find an answer."

"But he did communicate with you?" V'sair asked, filling a glass with liquid for her to drink.

"Yes." She paused, biting her lip. "It has something to do with Ereth, but what exactly, I just don't know."

V'sair nodded. "That flood was deliberate. Do you think the Elements are angry with us?"

"If they were, neither Tulani nor I would have survived. The Elements are never vengeful. You know that."

"But what could the flood signify?"

"I feel like I know; I just can't put my finger on it. If they meant to frighten me, they succeeded." Taking a shaky breath, she added, "I did not realize how long I haven't really used my gills. I have gotten lazy in the clouds."

"What use have you or anybody else for gills when you make your home in Syos? It makes no sense. I watched the whole flood from Hother's back, unable to do anything. If not for Bobbien and that captain, Seren, surely I would have perished trying to get to you."

"They have my eternal gratitude for keeping you from harm," Reminda said quietly.

"I have the bruises to show for it." V'sair smiled.

"Bobbien said only their strongest warrior was able to contain you." She motioned for him to sit beside her. "So, Tulani is finally here."

"Just in time for the coronation," he agreed. "I will make it a wedding ceremony?"

Reminda nodded regally. "It is time for you to start your dynasty. I just wish Zayden was here."

V'sair kissed his mother's forehead. "I must go, Mother. General Swart is waiting for me."

V'sair took the steps from his mother's apartments two at a time. She would be moving now, he knew. These would be Tulani's quarters within a few short weeks.

Both Swart and Vekin were waiting in his own chambers when he got there.

"You have told him?" V'sair asked the old man.

Vekin nodded but Swart spoke. "I cannot believe it.

How could he betray us?" He had seen the message revealing Chanter Brault as a traitor. It detailed a coming invasion, a Plantan invasion, engineered by both his uncles. Their unlikely alliance was as disturbing as their plans to replace Staf Nuen on the throne by getting rid of V'sair.

"The problem is, we don't know how deep-rooted is this decay."

"I want to arrest him!" Swart slammed his fist against the wall. "I will flay him alive!"

"Think, General—if we arrest him, we will never know who else is a part of this. We must see this thing through. What have you done, General Vekin?"

Vekin stood painfully, snapping his gnarled fingers so that a three-dimensional map sprang up to rotate in midair.

"We don't know where the attack will be, so I have spread our forces throughout the four continents. Division one is hidden on the lee side of Aqin." All three of them walked around the map, studying the placement of the troop. He indicated the slope of the great volcano and continued, "I have placed a regiment facing Hixom Sea. The third division, run by Seren, the new commander, is hidden in wait in the eastern provinces, and lastly, I have left the elite guards within the castle."

"Seren?" Swart asked.

"It's the new Quyroo infantry that we've created. I've given him a brevet command for his bravery in the flood. I've removed all Darracian commanders from the Quyroo forces, consolidating them into one huge fighting unit. Rather than facing the infighting within the ranks, we are keeping the two groups separate."

"Do you think that's wise?" V'sair asked, looking at a list of each unit and its commander.

Vekin shrugged. "I'd rather they fight the enemy than each other."

"A recipe for disaster!" Swart argued. "As it is, we are

spread too thin. You can't expect swords and spears to beat their guns! I wish I had cannon!"

"May I remind you, General, it was the Quyroos that stormed the castle and made it possible for us to put down the rebellion, without the aid of gunpowder. I know my uncle; he would never use cowardly means to retake Darracia. He will never be able to keep it that way. Besides, there is no missile or ammunition capable of penetrating our dense rocks." V'sair's blue eyes bore into General Swart.

"That may be so, Your Highness. You know my thoughts on the matter."

"I will go over the battle plans with each individual commander, but I fear to bring them together until we root out the traitors," Vekin added. "I know they are waiting. Waiting for a signal."

V'sair sighed. "As long as we remain a planet divided, there will not be peace within."

"As long as your uncle is on the loose, there will be no peace anywhere," Swart told him grimly.

♦

V'sair knocked gently on the door to Tulani's quarters. He was admitted by Bobbien, who smiled and said, "I go to your lady mother now. I must then return to the Desa. I have work to do, you know." She pressed her hand flat on his chest. "Are we friends again, Your Highness?"

"Don't ever do that to me again!" he told her sternly.

"You could have told Seren to let me go. I know a Quyroo will listen to a high priestess over a king."

"Things have changed in the Desa. I don't know if anyone hears me anymore. Besides, I changed your diapers, quite a few times." She chuckled. "You may be king, but to me, well, it is different."

"Greanam!" Tulani hissed. "Some respect for the king, if you please." She reached out to pull him deeper into the room, her lips moist and inviting. V'sair needed no more invitation.

They heard Bobbien's boisterous laughter all the way down the halls.

V'sair embraced Tulani, his lips kissing her temple, her cheek, then finally her lips. She moaned with pleasure, pulling his shirt free so their skin could touch. She ran her hand nimbly up his strong back. V'sair gasped with pleasure as their skin molded. He pushed his face into the soft skin of her neck and inhaled her fresh scent. Tears leaked from the corners of her eyes, and V'sair stopped to push her chin up.

"Tears?"

"I am happy…I feel whole once more." It was hard to speak with the king nuzzling her neck. She felt her skin come alive, tingling from head to toe, and wanted nothing more than to touch him all over.

He hugged her tightly. "I know. I know." Their lips met again for a soul-searing kiss that seemed to last forever. They parted for a second, their breathing harsh. "I have to stop, or I won't be able to…"

"I don't know if I want you to stop," Tulani whispered, her eyes bright pools of longing in her face.

"I have to go—there is a battle looming."

"A battle?"

"Yes. Staf is planning an invasion." He pulled her deeper into the room, his lips close to her ear. "There is a traitor." "Who?" Tulani searched his face.

"Chanter Brault."

"The chanter!" Tulani whispered. "Have you arrested him?"

V'sair pressed his fingers over her sensitive lips. "Not yet. We are waiting to flush out his accomplices. We are not sure where or when the invasion starts, but we are mobilizing."

"I am scared."

V'sair cupped her face. "One last battle and then we will be divided no more, not Darracian, not Quyroo. You and I"—he kissed her deeply—"will unite the planet and bring forth an age of peace and prosperity."

"But the battle-"

"Will be over and the threat gone. We will prevail, Tulani." He kissed her thoroughly, leaving her knees weak, her heart beating a frantic tattoo. She watched his broad shoulders longingly as he left the room.

She touched her bee-stung lips, the taste of him lingering.

"How do you know?" she managed to ask the empty room after he left.

XVIII

STAF WATCHED DARRACIA fill the screen as they entered the planet's atmosphere.

"We arrive," he said with satisfaction.

Lothen stood impatiently. "We have hours yet. I am waiting to hear from my contact. It is time to introduce you to Geva."

It had been cold between the two leaders since they captured Zayden. Lothen simmered about the remark Staf had made. Plantans had an excess of pride that rankled him. They walked together toward a room beyond Lothen's quarters.

It was larger than Staf expected. A caldron stood in the front, bloodstains dripping down its sides. Lothen motioned for Staf to stand next to him. Covering his face with his webbed hands, Lothen called out with weird clicks of his tongue, sounding much like the giant fish that swam in the Hixom Sea. The room was freezing, the frost clouding before their lips. A keening wail sounding like one hundred voices answered Lothen's call, filling the room so loudly that Staf covered his ears. Lights flashed; electric charges similar to jagged lightning sparked around the room, followed by kettle-like clanging so loud it hurt Staf's ears. It vibrated through his entire body, thumping in time to his startled heart. Staf was afraid he'd never hear again.

Lothen pulled out an X-shaped dagger and slit his palm from one end to another. His eyes were so glazed they appeared white. He held his hand in the air, cocked his head, and turned to Staf. Swiftly, without warning, he grabbed Staf's palm, slicing quickly, opening it as well. Staf hissed with pain, and would have slapped him, but the Plantan pressed their palms together. Instantly, they sizzled, and the room filled with the odor of burned flesh. A charge coursed between their bodies, sending them into a vortex of exquisite pain. Staf saw himself from outside his body, levitating, hand pressed to hand, as they began to spin in a dizzying circle. The room erupted into a kaleidoscope of neon colors, the light penetrating his retina to stain his brain. He heard wild laughter, wondered whose it was, and considered that this far exceeded any graphen vision he'd experienced. As they slowed, a black cloud gathered above them to settle over their heads, lazily changing into the shape of a woman, her head covered with a nest of squirming snakes. She had bottomless black pits for eyes, and a mouth with hundreds of sharp, pointed teeth. Staf closed his eyes from the pain of the scorched palms. He expected the vision to disappear when he reopened them. He heard her laughter first; it was an evil thing, raking through his head, clutching his heart. Staf's knees weakened, and his legs would have buckled if Lothen had not held him up.

"He is one of us, Geva." Lothen spoke triumphantly.

"Staf Nuen," she said, her voice a nasal whine. "We have waited for you to join our legions."

He felt the hot gaze of the monster on his face.

"You are a welcome addition to our army," she added. "The dark forces have been waiting for you."

Staf was speechless. He stared openmouthed, no words coming out.

"Kiss him, Lothen. Give him the kiss of Geva." The thing glowed red, the snakes on her head hissing and spitting.

Lothen grabbed his face, kissing him full on the lips. Staf felt his breath sucked out of his mouth, his body emptying completely. His knew his blood was gone, his bones so brittle that if touched, they would turn to dust. His head was hollow, his skin a dry shell covering his depleted body. From sightless eyes, he watched Geva grow until she took up the entire room. Lothen still held his face, his palms caressing his numb cheeks, an evil smile on his face. Taking a deep breath, Staf felt himself fill up with the fetid air and knew he was back, but something was different.

"You and I are one," Lothen told him. "Your soul belongs to Geva. We will rule the galaxy in her name."

He released Staf, whose boneless body weakly leaned against a wall.

Lothen turned to the revolting creature. "Thy will is done." He knelt reverently. Glancing up at Staf, he said plainly, "Kneel. Kneel to your new goddess and know in her hands is your destiny."

XIX

"WHAT HAPPENED?" ZAYDEN groaned as he sat up. "Did I pass out?"

"Like a little girl." Denita rolled her eyes. "You better?"

Zayden got up slowly and rolled off the cot to examine the door for a way out.

"Yes, we have to get out of here."

"My sister is going to get us out."

"How do you know?" Zayden walked the perimeters of the room, looking for escape routes.

"She's my sister; she is eminently resourceful," Denita told him, as if that would be enough.

Zayden hauled himself up to open a vent. It was stuck fast. He searched the room, looking for something to pry it open.

"What do you need?" Denita asked.

"Something sharp," Zayden said absently.

The door rattled, then opened, Naje framed in the hallway, her face tense with fear. "This way…" she urged.

They raced through the corridors, toward a landing bay, through the lower decks of the ship.

"You have but a small window of time," Naje told them breathlessly over her shoulder. "Leave Darracia. Go back toward Venturian. Forget this place."

Zayden shook his head. "I can't. My family is here. It is my home. I have to help them."

"He may have to, but you don't." She locked her gaze with her sister's. "They will be destroyed."

Zayden shook his head. "The rocks of Darracia are too thick. Nothing will affect them. Your artillery is useless."

"It's not my artillery; this is not my fight. Lothen will call on Geva, and she will crush Darracia." They hid in a hallway, watching guards patrol.

"Geva?" Zayden asked.

"The opposite of your Elements. She is the essence of evil." She looked at Denita. "He goes to certain death if he returns to the planet surface. You could stay here with me."

"Nothing is for certain." Denita touched her arm. "You would choose slavery?"

Naje placed her hands on her abdomen. "I choose Staf Nuen."

"I don't understand you!"

"Shush! They will hear you."

"Come with us," Denita pleaded.

"I cannot." Naje shook her head. "Whatever the

outcome, my fate is tied to Staf Nuen." She kissed her sister on the cheek, then pointed to the door to the landing bay.

XX

LOTHEN'S EYES GLEAMED with icy resolution. He stood on the deck of the ship, Staf next to him, and gave the command for the three ships to begin their invasion. His communication officer interrupted his thought.

"Highness…"

"Yes?"

"It is the holy man, Brault." He pressed his earpiece tightly to the side of his head, listening through the static. "He is afraid they've been found out. They have captured some spies…The first cell is dead. Every member."

"Just the first cell?"

The officer typed in a response. "He says he never met the others. He can't swear that they are all in position."

Lothen grunted, then nodded to the navigator to begin their descent.

The three triangular ships began slowly descending

onto the choppy surface of the water. Plantan strategy was to land on the Hixom Sea and bombard the city of Syos as well as the Desa. The population would gladly give up their weak king in order to have peace. He would install his puppet, Staf Nuen, on the throne, load him up with graphen, and strip Darracia of its resources. A smile of malice split Lothen's face.

"Do you give warning?" Staf asked.

"What would be the fun in that?" Lothen laughed.

"The Elements may react."

"Let them try. That is why I have Geva! Let's say hello to our new friends. On my command, begin the bombardment."

"You mean to bomb? I thought this would be a raid," Staf asked Lothen. "Darracia can withstand any siege—the city walls are impenetrable. Gunpower means nothing to us."

"I don't remember discussing strategies with you, my lord Nuen," he answered frostily.

"We never talked using guns. You said it would be like your raids on Venturian." Staf's face was red with anger.

Lothen stood with both hands reaching the ceiling. "Geva! Silence this fool!"

Staf choked, grabbing his neck, the veins popping from lack of breath. His feet left the floor as he was held up like a wet puppy to be shaken ruthlessly. Lothen snapped his webbed fingers, and Staf collapsed to his knees, breathing hard. "The Elements...the Elements do not allow..."

"To hell with your Elements! You have sold your

soul to Geva; to you, the Elements do not exist," Lothen shouted, his mouth foaming. He came close to Staf, taking his shirt in both hands. "Are you with me or against me?" he asked with a lethalness that chilled Staf.

Staf swallowed. "With you."

Lothen turned to his gunner and screamed, "Prepare to fire."

The orders were echoed, guns were aimed at the castle, and Lothen, calm once more, told his gunner, "Commence to fire."

XXI

V'SAIR HEARD ABOUT the formation of three Plantan ships landing on the Hixom Sea. He raced to the Orbitus Chamber and met up with both Vekin and Swart, his hands on his hips, deep in thought. "Did they ask permission to land?"

The room had been turned into a command center. Uniformed officers rushed in and out of the chamber, relaying messages to the various commanders. Giant screens floated in the air, static interfering with transmissions. V'sair saw Seren's worried face, explosions rocking the ground underneath him.

"What's going on?" V'sair demanded.

"They've fired on us," Vekin responded, then turned to give instructions to an aide.

"Fired on us? They are using guns?" V'sair asked incredulously.

"We have had no communication with them," Swart added.

"Have you tracked their radio signals?"

"They are trading dialogue with—"

The walls of the palace shook as a salvo blasted against its surface but did little damage.

"What are they using?" V'sair watched the missiles hit the surrounding buildings, but the red rock was dense— strong enough to withstand their firepower.

"It's old but can be quite lethal for the Desa, and our population," Vekin told him. "I will have two battalions head toward them."

"With what?" Swart yelled. "We will be obliterated. We are no match to their guns."

"The stone walls of Darracia will withstand their ammunition," V'sair said with finality.

"Our skin will not deflect their bullets!"

"It is the Desa I am worried about. Can we evacuate the Quyroos?" V'sair asked urgently.

Vekin shook his head. "Not enough time. I have sent soldiers in to guide them as deep into the Desa as they can go. Many of the older ones are stubborn and won't leave. You know how they are."

"It is their home. Bombardment is unprecedented," V'sair replied. "This is an abomination."

Swart growled, "I told you we should have bought the cannon the Pagilans offered to sell us."

V'sair ignored the older man, then glanced at the giant screen, feeling his mother's presence before she said anything. They stood together in mute horror, watching the enemy ships lob bombs into the vulnerable forests.

"Have you tried talking to them?" she asked quietly.

V'sair shook his head. The screens lit up with Quyroos running wildly from their burning homes, scrambling through the trees to escape.

"Return all the shuttles to the Desa to evacuate as many as you can," V'sair ordered.

"Sire, you may as well paint a target on their backs. The shuttles will just condense people into obvious groups for them to shoot."

"We have to do something."

"Let me go down there and speak to him," Reminda told him, her hand on his arm in appeal.

"No, Mother." He winced as another shot echoed off the strong rock wall of his fortress. He watched a spray of sparks ricochet. "It is too dangerous."

"He is my brother."

"You hardly know him."

"He is still my brother."

"I can't allow it," V'sair told her with finality.

The room was filling up with additional members of the high command. V'sair could hear his experts rapping out orders. The latest battle for Darracia had begun in earnest.

Swart came over to him and said quietly, "It is time for us to take Brault in."

"We still don't know who he is associated with."

"It hardly matters now." Swart shook his head. "He is an enemy that must be contained."

V'sair nodded in agreement and watched Swart direct his men to take the chanter into custody.

♦

Tulani looked on in wide-eyed shock as fires ripped through the Desa. Felise whimpered beside her, resting her paws on the balustrade.

"You shouldn't be out here." V'sair rested his hand on the small of her back. She turned to face him, grim faced. "Have you heard from Bobbien?"

She shook her head, a silver tear tracking down her red cheeks.

"I am sure she's fine," V'sair assured her. "I have sent my personal guard to find her."

"She is hiding from the flames. If I know her, she went inland, deep into the Desa. How many Quyroos have been killed?" she asked thickly.

"We don't have any numbers yet." He paused. "If I had known they were going to bomb, we would have evacuated the population earlier."

"Nobody expected it. I shall go down to help."

"Afterward, Tulani. We will both go down to help."

XXII

SIRENS ERUPTED ALL over the ship. Lothen turned toward his communication officer with a question on his face. "What's going on?"

"The prisoners have escaped." He held his device close to his ear, nodded, and added, "They are heading to the landing bay."

Staf grabbed his Fireblade from his side and responded, "I will kill the devil's whelp, once and for all." He stormed out of the room to finish his fight with Zayden.

Zayden, Denita, and Naje stood in the corridor, waiting for an opportunity to reach the escape door. Naje turned to her sister and said, "This is where we part." They embraced. She turned to Zayden. "Take care of her, Warrior, or I will find you."

Zayden smiled, taking Denita's hand, ready to sprint

toward his ship. He spun, coming face-to-face with his uncle, Fireblade drawn.

Zayden backed off, raising his pistol.

"You would fight me like a coward?" Staf asked silkily.

Zayden held the gun, Staf in his sights.

"Pull the trigger, Zayden!" Denita screamed.

Naje withdrew a volatile packet of graphen from under her shirt. She watched Zayden raise his weapon and yelled, "No!" throwing the small explosive to smash against the wall next to him. Upon impact, it exploded, tossing Zayden like a rag doll to land in a heap on the floor.

Staf shook his head, dazed from the explosion, saw Zayden prone on the ground, and stalked over to fillet him with his angry blade.

"Why did you do that?" Staf turned on her. "I had him." As he raised his sword for the kill, she stilled his arm. "Leave him." She gestured to the dying man. "He is finished. Blinded. See?" She pointed to Zayden's bloody face.

"Let him suffer."

"I have to finish this!" Staf shook himself free.

"Lothen will steal the throne. I know him. You must go to the deck, before he takes your birthright." She placed his palm on her abdomen. "Your son's birthright."

Staf looked down at her, his yellow eyes brightening. "You are sure?"

Naje shook her head. "Yes."

He grabbed her hand. "Come with me."

Naje put her arm through his and began walking toward the deck. Discreetly, she made eye contact with

Denita, hidden in the shadows. She mouthed, "He lives. Get to safety."

Rolling her eyes, she motioned to the escape route, Zayden's ship just past the door.

Denita watched in mute shock as her sister hustled out of the area, Staf Nuen's arm around her. Getting on her knees, she surveyed the wreck of a man and pulled him unsteadily to his feet. "Let's get out of here."

Somehow, Denita pushed and prodded Zayden into the backseat. Fingers fumbling, she belted him in. She took his face between her palms, surveying the damage. He was a bloody mess. She tried lifting his eyelid, but it was glued tight with blood. Zayden brushed her hands away with a deep moan. After sliding down the skin of the ship, she ran to a console with a board full of switches. She considered their colors and chose what she thought would be the correct control, watching in awe as the rear cargo doors parted. A blast of cold, wet air hit her in the face, and she saw they were hovering over the choppy gray sea. She hoisted herself into Zayden's bucket seat, looked at all the switches, shrugged, then started flipping everything into the on position. The radio blasted, lights blinked, and the pretty little craft jumped up to do a little spin, making her dizzy. She heard sirens and once again looked at the door in time to see a group of Plantans burst through, guns drawn and aimed at her.

"Here goes nothing!" she told no one in particular as she punched the throttle and backed into them, spilling them like toy soldiers. There were screams and a few shots.

Ducking instinctively, she twisted the knob in the other direction, projecting out of the Plantan ship like a shot. Soaring over the water, she felt the engines stall, and, cursing, she heard Zayden's weak voice.

"Use the red handle."

Looking back, she saw his bloody face—his good eye was closed, his breathing raspy.

"What?"

"The red is up; blue is down…Get it?" He turned white; his head rolled to the side.

She pushed the red throttle, smiling as the ship took off almost perpendicular to the raging sea. In the distance, she saw the walls of a beautiful city under bombardment but still amazingly whole. She knew she couldn't fly into the line of fire, so using the wheel, she turned sharply toward a giant volcano rising from a smoking red forest.

XXIII

THE BATTLE RAGED. By nightfall, many buildings were pitted by the attack but standing as strong and as solid as they had in the morning. Using ships, the Darracians sent their whole first division to attempt to board the enemy in the Hixom Sea. V'sair watched in horror as they were picked off to drown, their boats never even getting close to the alien vessels. Parts of the Desa burned; the beaches were littered with Seren's soldiers, killed in the second attempt to repel the invasion.

"This is getting nowhere." V'sair turned to his staff. "They are destroying the Desa. I will go and talk to them."

"They will kill you, and where would we be!" Swart growled. "Syos is safe."

"But the Desa is not," V'sair said miserably.

"Look." Vekin pointed to a screen showing a slender body picking her way through the carnage to reach the sea. V'sair looked at one of the many screens and realized his mother was on the beach.

"Mother," V'sair whispered despairingly, turning to follow her.

"V'sair, wait." Vekin stopped him. "Let her do this. Perhaps she can talk some sense into them. They are her species, after all."

"She is unprotected." V'sair shook his head. "Prepare Hother."

"You cannot leave, sire!" Vekin held his arm.

"This is madness. I should be there. I must be the one to negotiate with them."

"You can't negotiate with the devil!" Swart yelled. "That fat bag of wind Brault hasn't talked! We don't know who the other traitors are!"

"It doesn't matter anymore. All is lost. At least if I go to them, perhaps I can make things easier for Darracia and my people."

"You go to certain death," Vekin told him.

"In life nothing is certain except for death." V'sair ran to the stables.

◆

Reminda slid down the embankment, her white hair a beacon to her brother, who watched with interest as she approached the sandy beach.

Lothen sent a small craft for his sister and waited for her in his quarters. It was quiet now. They didn't know that he had used up most of his firepower. He was running low on ammunition. The damn city remained as upright and whole as when he started. He looked upward, calling out to Geva, his eyes hot pits of coal.

"Geva," he demanded, "does the Element have more power than you! Make these bastards fall." He pounded his chest. "My time has come! It is our covenant. Forsake not your most cherished follower."

The air around him churned, enveloping him in a gray mist, followed by a foul odor. "You dare question my power?" He heard Geva's voice fill the room. Pressure grew, and Lothen fell to his knees as if he had been slammed to the floor. "I lust for blood. Bring me blood, and I will bring you Darracia!"

"Geva commanded." Lothen bowed his head. "And I obey." He rose to look at the bombarded city in the sky, the black skyline of the burning forest. "So, Geva says it won't be long now. They have lost; we have conquered them." He didn't even think he needed his puppet, Staf Nuen, anymore. He had watched Staf preening over the slave, calling her his queen. It disgusted him, but what did he expect—the man was a graphen addict and in the thrall of the Venturian slave. He would make a gift to Geva of that one.

The door opened, and he saw his sister pushed in. He bowed with a sneer. "Ah, the mighty Reminda. Your son is not man enough to do his work."

Reminda walked in, furious. "He is ten times the man you are. He wouldn't kill innocents!"

Lothen grabbed her by her forearms, his face purple with rage. "There are no innocents!"

"Why are you doing this?"

"Oh, high-and-mighty Reminda, the good and generous queen. When did you think of anybody but your precious Drakko or Darracia? Did you ever think to do something for your homeland?"

"I asked…We tried…"

"Not hard enough."

"Father put a price on my head. What did you expect me to do?" Reminda spat. "What did you expect me to do?"

"I know what I am going to do." He pressed his intercom and threw her toward two guards who entered. "My sister wants a new career. Put her in a pod. She goes to Bina to work in the mines."

Lothen stalked past her white face, turning to sneer before he left, "Now I go to finish your son."

◆

V'sair rode Hother to the banks of the great ocean, his army below, his cavalry behind him. Dressed all in blue, with the flag of Darracia held by Swart's grandson, his standard-bearer, he approached the ships bobbing on the water. The sea had turned an odd shade of purple, swirling foam covering the choppy waves. He realized with a start, his two uncles stood united on the enemy ship, looking to overtake his home.

"Lothen?" he called out, his voice ringing through the fog.

"Here." A tall man with a war knot of ivory hair

moved in front. "Greetings, Nephew." He bowed, a mocking glint in his blue eyes. "I bring you tidings from your home planet."

"Darracia is my home planet." V'sair nodded in acknowledgement. "Where is my mother?"

"She is safe."

"I didn't ask you that! Where is she?"

"It is of no consequence. We have won. Your Elements have changed sides. Geva is the new religion here."

"What do you want from us?" V'sair called out.

Lothen laughed, smiling as a stallius cantered toward the king. "Took you long enough." He spoke to the Quyroo riding toward the king, his voice carrying over the distance.

"I was detained; forgive me, sire." Seren jumped off his stallius to kneel toward the ship. He pointed a gun at V'sair's heart. "You are invited to join your uncles on the ship, V'sair," he sneered.

Fireblades were drawn as two Darracian soldiers jumped from their mounts.

"Do anything, and your king dies." Seren turned to V'sair. "They have your mother. King Lothen has told me to tell you that if you do anything, she will die, and die painfully."

"Seren! Why? We gave you a command of your own." Seren walked over to V'sair. "You poached on the Quyroo preserve. Tulani will never be yours."

V'sair slid off Hother and gave the reins to his standardbearer. "Take her." He followed Seren to the launch to take him to the Plantan ship.

XXIV

THE SMALL CRAFT careened over the smoking forest, bumping into trees. With each thump, she heard Zayden groan painfully.

Denita scanned for a patch of meadow or grass to attempt a landing. It was all just one jumble of red; she could barely distinguish anything in the gloom. The ship lurched, the wing clipped by an outcropping of rocks, sending it into a spin. Bile rose to the back of Denita's throat when they rotated upside down to hang suspended for a minute before the engines died and they began to spiral down. Locking her arms rigidly, she wrestled with the wheel, trying to right the craft, but it wouldn't budge

The monochromatic wall of trees sped past her, tears gathering in her eyes at her and Zayden's helplessness. Something grabbed the ship, halting it in a springlike motion, and it bounced nauseatingly in a trap, rocking as if in a cradle.

The motion slowed, the ship still bouncing, her stomach rushing up to meet her gullet. Zayden was ominously quiet. Denita unbuckled herself to check on Zayden. Fumbling with his latch, she tried to lift it, but it was stuck fast. On her knees, she pounded with her fists, but it was immovable.

She felt a hot hand touch her shoulder, and she screamed, turning to see a wizened creature curiously looking at her. Naked from the waist up, she was wrinkled and red, with star-shaped eyes examining her.

"Bobbien help?" she asked in a musical voice.

Denita opened her mouth, but no sounds came out. The odd creature looked in the backseat and spied the injured Darracian.

"Oh my, Zayden. What have you done to yourself?" Bobbien climbed onto the craft, making it feel even more unstable. She considered Denita's white face. "Don't look down, dearie. It's a long trip."

Denita turned to gaze at the drop, swallowing compulsively.

"I told you not to look down," Bobbien admonished.

"Help me."

Her long red fingers were able to loosen the glass hatch, and she watched, slack-jawed, as the old woman pulled Zayden from the wreckage with unbelievable strength.

"Come!" She held out a hand to the younger girl. "Follow me. I fix him, no?"

Denita reached out and let this alien creature guide her to safety.

XXV

SEREN HUSTLED V'SAIR into the knee-deep water to board the skiff sent out to them. They climbed in, and V'sair turned to the Quyroo. "Not two days ago, you saved my life."

"I had to. I was being watched. Bobbien was right behind me."

"I don't understand…" V'sair said quietly.

"There is nothing to understand. As long as you are king, the most I can hope is to serve you, rise to some inconsequential post in the army. Lothen made me a better offer."

"But he is Plantan."

"So are you," Seren responded, then looked to the red stone city floating in the clouds above them.

Seren pushed V'sair none too gently as they boarded the painted Plantan vessel. It bobbed in the unsteady water, and V'sair reached out to hold a rail. Seren shoved him hard in the shoulder, directing him to Lothen's quarters. Inside, Staf stood next to Lothen, a dark-eyed woman next to him. The room was icy cold; V'sair shivered in spite of himself. Lothen drank from a clear goblet—a small red fish swam inside. V'sair heard faint mewing, but could not find its source.

"So, now you have both my mother and me. What do you want, ransom? Crystals?" V'sair asked.

Staf stepped forward. "Your reign is finally over. You and that Plantan whore can orbit the planet for the rest of your miserable lives. Now Darracia will have justice."

"You will never rule Darracia. Ozre will stop you," V'sair replied defiantly.

Lothen eased his lanky frame from his chair, taking his goblet with him. He walked close to V'sair, towering over him. He raised his glass with a salute, and V'sair watched in horror as he downed a small humanoid creature.

"Delicious…Would you like some?" Lothen asked with his basilisk stare. "You are Plantan—you might like it."

"Half Plantan," V'sair said distastefully. "I prefer Darracian customs."

"You are a rare mixture, a regular ambassador for all species." Lothen walked around the room. "Your mother is Plantan; your father Darracian; you love a Quyroo." He stopped and grabbed V'sair by his chin. "I know everything about you, Nephew; you sip from every flower, taking only what you want. Do you have gills, V'sair?"

"No," V'sair answered curtly. "This is no business of yours."

Lothen grabbed his hand. "No gills, no webs between your fingers, yet you are shaped like us." He pulled the sleeve up his arm roughly to examine the bluish skin.

V'sair pulled away. "I am Darracian in body and anima. If this is your idea of what makes a Plantan, I am happy to say the only thing I have in common with you is my mother.

Where is she?" he demanded.

"She is no longer your concern."

"If you have harmed her, I will kill you."

Lothen laughed. Staf shifted from one foot to the other impatiently. "Kill him and get it over with."

Lothen ignored him, walking over to consider V'sair again.

"I just want to know if you are more Plantan than Darracian." His uncle circled him, watching the younger man. He touched the white braid, and V'sair defiantly pulled away. "You are not in a position to be arrogant. Try it," Lothen commanded as he brought another goblet with a fish swimming frantically around in a circle.

V'sair realized the mewing sound was coming from its frightened mouth.

His uncle held the glass to his lips, forcing V'sair to drink. "Try it, V'sair. You might like it, and us. Try it and we can talk about a proposition," his oily voice wheedled.

V'sair looked away, his eyes scanning his ruined forests through the portholes.

"What!" Staf interrupted. "You didn't say anything about this!"

"I don't remember that I have to report to you.

Meanwhile, I see two kings here, not three."

Staf stalked over to him and put his face very close to Lothen's. "This was not our deal."

Lothen touched the older man's neck and replied, "Don't let me call on Geva." He turned to Seren. "Take them out of here and lock them up."

Seren paused, looking at both men. Lothen laughed, reaching out to touch the Quyroo on the shoulder. "Oh, don't worry, Seren. Both the Desa and Tulani are yours."

Seren grabbed Staf, and another guard used his gun to push them out the door.

"Come sit by me, Nephew." Lothen eyed his sister's son with interest. "They say you are the new Darracia. Why?"

V'sair looked out the ports of the room. "What does it matter now that you will destroy it?"

"I have no need to do that. I merely need a new place to make my home."

"You came with Nuen."

"He is a graphen addict. Oh yes, he is far gone and useless. We could do great things together."

"Your Geva and the Elements will not coexist together. They are fundamentally different."

"Yes, V'sair, you are right." He spun and shouted to the room, "Do you hear that, Geva? You can't coexist with Darracia's precious Elements. What do you think of that!"

The air rippled around them, almost gelling. V'sair felt the oxygen being sucked out of his lungs. A small whirlpool started over Lothen's head, filling the room with rushing air. It swirled around the room, caressing him with its slimy heat, then narrowed to a long, thin stream to fly out the window. Once outside, it grew into a huge black cloud, filling the sky to skirt through the buildings. It looked like a living thing, expanding and contracting, covering whole areas, obliterating the skyline, and taking a leisurely route to the volcano. The giant mass settled on the beach. V'sair watched his soldiers look up as it blanketed them like a black blizzard. There were muffled shouts, followed by blood-curdling screams, and then a stillness that screamed louder than sound.

The dense thing lifted, leaving the beach strewn with bodies, their gray faces bleached white and bloodless. V'sair gripped the back of a chair, then turned to his uncle. "You are despicable, pure evil."

Lothen bowed his head, a smirk on his lips, as if V'sair had bestowed a compliment. "Thank you. I do try my best."

V'sair turned to attack, and Lothen froze him with his next sentence. "Try it, and Geva will smother your city in the clouds. Oh, look. She engages with your Ozre."

They turned to see fire spitting from the roof of Aqin, the sky darkening with the ash spewing out of its cone. The vaporous being moved aggressively toward the volcano, and V'sair watched in astonishment as it expanded to cover the entirety of the huge mountain. The atmosphere clouded with sulfuric fumes, while a battle raged behind the screen of the entity that cocooned the majestic volcano. An explosion rent the air, rocks flying, huge plumes of fire, and for a minute V'sair felt the relief of knowing Ozre had overcome the enemy. A second explosion, followed by the racket of thousands of rocks hitting the walls of the volcano, deafened the air, echoing back at them.

Lothen laughed like a wild thing. "You think Ozre will triumph over Geva? Watch, V'sair, and understand you never stood a chance."

The sky slowly cleared to reveal Aqin hollowed out, broken like a weak tooth, reduced to a great pile of rubble. Shaken to his knees, V'sair sank onto a chair, turned to his uncle, and said in the barest whisper, "Do what you want to me, but leave the people alone."

Lothen threw back his head, roaring with laughter that shook the very rafters of the ship.

"I will not help you," V'sair told Lothen in a low voice.

"Then you will die." Lothen walked out of the silent room.

♦

Naje waited until they stepped out of an elevator before she flicked two graphen packets behind her, shoving Staf before her so they wouldn't get caught in the explosion. Seren flew backward into the lift, the wind knocked out of him, losing consciousness when a guard fell on top of him. Staf stumbled, and Naje grabbed his hand, but not before relieving a dead guard of his firearms.

She threw one to Staf, who deftly caught it. "I will not use this!"

"Oh, grow up!" she shouted back. Turning, she fired on three Plantans running toward them, their guns drawn. "Let's get off this ship."

"I will not run. I was promised the throne."

"Lothen's forked tongue talks two ways. We have to get out of here!"

They ran to the pod level, squeezed into the tiny escape vehicle, and Naje ejected them out of their enemies' clutches and into the unknown.

XXVI

BOBBIEN COVERED THE young Darracian's eye with the sap of the caylet tree, but held little hope. He was awake but not speaking. She liked the girl and her devotion, but the hulking young man was shriveling up. She had no time for his self-pity.

Bobbien had set up a base of sorts under the low-hanging trees of the eastern provinces. They were surrounded by the muddy quicksand, and if a body didn't know its way, it would be swallowed by one of the many sinkholes and end up roasting in the thermal springs underneath. She glanced up sadly at the ruined face of Aqin. So many dead, so many, she thought sadly. This was indeed a dark day for Darracia and its people. Soon, the Quyroos would find her, and she would help them. They would be rebels, for she knew V'sair was gone. Perhaps this one, Drakko's other son, would lead them to victory. When he woke up to stop feeling sorry for himself and realized he could do everything he needed to without his sight, he would be their savior. Yes, Bobbien thought, he would lead them to victory against the advancing evil.

◆

Reminda looked out the tiny pod window and watched the stars speed by. She was no longer shackled; she didn't need to be. She was a prisoner, programed to meet up with a prison ship where she would be transported to land in Bina. She would be destined to live on the cliffs, her name forgotten, only a number to identify her when death claimed her. Her only comfort was that then, and only then, she would be joined to Drakko forever. She only hoped it would not be too long.

◆

Staf and Naje flew toward a new unknown, homeless, friendless, and without any idea of how or when they would come back. But the one thing they both knew with certainty was they would return to destroy Lothen and take the throne.

◆

V'sair walked toward the metal cage, his hands tied behind his back. Seren stood by the control device, a giant bruise covering half his face.

Lothen stood on the highest point of the ship, a

speaker in his hand. "Behold, Darracia, your king will be dead.

Long live Lothen!"

The air was still. Crowds of Quyroos watched silently from the treetops, their red faces barely distinguishable from the foliage.

Darracians lined up on the balustrades; Generals Swart and Vekin, broken old men, watched helplessly as their king was escorted to his destiny. V'sair looked for the face he wanted imprinted on his final memory. When he saw her stricken look, their eyes locked, and for a second, no one existed but them. Tulani shook her head, her hands covering her mouth in mute shock.

V'sair walked to the golden cage, stepped inside, and held out his tied hands. "Surely I don't need to go to my death shackled. One prison is enough?"

Lothen looked at his nephew. "Your bravery does you credit. Untie him!"

"But sire!" Seren interrupted.

Lothen turned a fierce glare on the Quyroo. "I said untie him, else you will join him in his watery death."

The ropes were cut away, and V'sair solemnly stepped into the stark jail. The door clanged loudly behind him, and he faced outward toward his home, seeing only Tulani. His lips formed the words "I love you."

The nasal whine of the winch echoed over the water as V'sair was lowered into the lapping waves. He refused to look down. Soon the icy water chilled his body as it closed over his legs, his waist, and finally his head.

Tulani's wail of horror carried long after the water covered his hair.

Automatically he held his breath, his eyes closed, waiting for the last bubble to escape so he would sink into nothingness. His head got light, his arms floating within the cage, his body weightless. V'sair's breath hitched, and he released a final exhalation, feeling his lungs fill with water, and a peacefulness surrounded him. He heard music, ethereal and beautiful, angels singing. It was a holy choir, and in his mind's eye, he saw a white light coming closer. It split into two globes of light, one with a red center, the other blue. Reaching for it, he felt the last of his air escape and then nothing more.

The cage sank slowly to rest on the deep ocean floor. The young king lay in the ripples and eddies, small fish swimming around him. His tunic lifted, billowing out in the gentle wave of the water. The two orbs hovered over him, expanding to surround him, caress him, invade his still form. V'sair's body became incandescent, the inner lights of the blue and red balls shining from his chest. A pulse started in his neck, his heart warming to the light of the orbs. The tight skin of his sides split. One, two, three slits appeared, opening like gentle flowers, bubbles of air filling the young king. Slowly the tiny gills struggled to move. Unused, underdeveloped, they worked hard to breathe, and then they did. V'sair's eyes popped open.

9 781947 118751